ANTIQUES, ARTIFACTS & ALIBIS

A Dogwood Springs Cozy Mystery

SALLY BAYLESS

Kimberlin Belle Publishing

Paperback ISNB: 978-1-946034-21-2

Kimberlin Belle Publishing

Contact: admin@kimberlinbelle.com

Publisher's Note: This is a work of fiction. Names, characters, places, and incidents are a product of the author's imagination. Locales and public names are sometimes used for atmospheric purposes. Any resemblance to actual people, living or dead, or to businesses, companies, events, institutions, or locales is completely coincidental.

Cover art by DLR Cover Designs, www.dlrcoverdesigns.com.

Chapter One

I SPENT the last leg of my trip from Philly, driving southwest from St. Louis to Dogwood Springs, trying not to get pinned in between semis and second-guessing my move to a small town in Missouri.

At first, when I got the job in Dogwood Springs, I'd been excited. But somewhere along the drive out—maybe in Indiana—doubts had set in. What if moving here was a mistake?

Over the past couple of years, I'd made a lot of mistakes. When I first noticed things beginning to sour in my marriage, I ignored the problem, focusing all my attention on my job as visitor services coordinator at the Henry C. Branch House, a prestigious colonial-era home and museum in Philadelphia.

After Reggie admitted he'd been cheating on me and said he wanted a divorce, I blundered on, numbed by the pain of having to work every day at the museum with both him and his girlfriend, a woman eight years younger than me and nine years younger than Reggie. Worse yet, probably because I was trying to avoid being around him, I didn't pick up on the fact that as time passed, Reggie was busy convincing our boss, the owner of the Branch House, that my position was no longer in line with the current mission of the organization. In January, a month after our divorce was final, I was out of a job. A few weeks later, Reggie's girlfriend got a massive promotion to a position almost identical to my previous job.

And, as a final massive misstep, I allowed the divorce and the job loss to shake my confidence so deeply that I flubbed my one chance at a great new job, the interview I managed to get at the Smithsonian.

So, yeah, a lot of mistakes.

Mistakes that left me, newly single Libby Ballard, on my own, starting over as the director of a small history museum in Dogwood Springs, Missouri, my mother's hometown.

Not where I'd hoped to be professionally when I hit thirty-two.

About ten miles from Dogwood Springs, I drew in a deep breath and raised my chin. For better or worse, the decision was made. I'd felt excited about the position when I was here for the interview. Maybe all this uncertainty was simply nerves.

I left Interstate 44 and pulled into town with three bulging suitcases, a few pieces of furniture, a stereo system with a turntable that had belonged to my dad in college, a mountain of cardboard moving boxes, and my mother's family pearls, which she'd given me when I turned twenty-one. With the help of GPS, I managed to drive the U-Haul and my silver Camry, which I was pulling on a hitch, down the narrow side streets to my new apartment, the ground floor of a plain, two-story house built in 1900.

My new place wasn't anything fancy, but Dogwood Springs did hold promise. The community, known as "the prettiest town in Missouri," was a tourist mecca. People came to see the springs, to stay at the quaint bed and breakfasts, to visit the nearby winery, and to shop and dine in the beautiful downtown.

Even Elm Street, where I'd be living, was quite nice. The street was lined with older homes, some lovingly refurbished, and some, like the house I would share with an upstairs neighbor, that could use some TLC. But no matter how fancy the house, the yards and porches were filled with color. Even my simple rental had a pot of black-eyed Susans and purple petunias by the mailbox. Well-established trees shaded the sidewalk on both sides of the street, offering relief from the summer heat.

After popping the last of my Advil, I helped the movers —three teenage grandsons of a friend of my mom's who happened to be free this first Saturday in June—unload the van. When the one who was in college offered me a lift back from the van drop-off spot, I gratefully accepted. Once we returned to my new apartment, I tipped him an extra twenty and went inside, trying to picture myself living in the space.

A small entryway opened to a door to my unit and stairs

to the second floor. My front door led into the living room, and I had one bedroom off to the right. A bathroom and closet were located behind the bedroom, and the kitchen, with a door to the backyard, was behind the living room. A window unit air-conditioner chugged away in one of the tall living room windows. Not central air, but it seemed to be doing the job. And the place was spotless. Not even a cobweb on a light fixture. Believe me, I'm no fan of spiders, so I checked.

It wasn't much space, but it was bigger than the apartment I'd gotten when my husband and I separated. At the time, I'd let my ex keep the bigger pieces, bargaining for some of the better small antiques, like the marble-topped table I used as my nightstand.

After looking around, I emptied a single box, the one marked "essentials," which held my favorite black tea, imported from Yorkshire, England, along with a mug, my tea kettle, bedding, shower curtain and towels, toilet paper, and a package of shortbread cookies I'd brought along for emergencies.

At that point, the thought of going to the store for groceries and opening boxes to find dishes was out of the question. I searched the Internet, found a pizza place, and ordered a thin-crust mushroom and black olive and, with a slight nod to good health, a house salad. Maybe after some dinner, I'd rebound and make a grocery run.

I called to let my mom and dad know I'd arrived safely and collapsed onto one of the few large pieces of furniture

I'd hauled from Philly, the couch my ex and I had once bought for our family room.

Half an hour later, a knock on the door from the entryway jerked me awake.

I blinked, startled by the unfamiliar sight of the cardboard boxes filling my new home. I was almost positive I'd locked the door from the outside to the entryway. I dug my wallet from the bottom of my oversized purse and peeked out the narrow window beside my front door.

A blond woman about my age stood in the entryway, holding a stack of napkins, a small salad container, and a pizza box. Not one of those thermal pizza carriers, just the box.

Odd.

I opened the door. "Hi. What do I owe you?"

"Nothing." She grinned at me. "I'm Cleo Anderson, your housemate. I just got home and saw the delivery guy. I haven't even been upstairs yet." Her words bubbled out as she handed me the pizza box, salad, and napkins.

"Oh, thanks. Libby Ballard." I tapped my chest. "Let me pay you."

"Nah, we're good. Hold on, I've got a housewarming gift for you."

Cleo darted up the stairs to her apartment, and her golden retriever wriggled its way into my living room.

I flipped over the one cardboard box I'd emptied, positioned it near the couch as a makeshift coffee table, and set the pizza box on top.

Cleo's dog rubbed my leg until I petted it, then sniffed near the pizza box.

I told it a firm "No."

It walked away from the pizza and made quick work of checking every room of my apartment. Returning to the living room, it tipped its head at me, perhaps wondering where Cleo had gone, and flopped down in front of the fireplace.

"I'm back," Cleo called out loudly.

I hurried to the entry and found her standing at my door with her arms full.

She handed me a bag that held a half gallon of milk, butter, a loaf of bread, a dozen eggs, and a jar of peanut butter, then followed me into the kitchen and held up a bottle of pinot noir and two red Solo cups. "Welcome to 406 South Elm Street."

A rush of warmth filled my chest. "Wow. Thank you." I loaded the perishables into the fridge, truly touched by the welcome.

Over the past year, I'd gone through some lonely times. My ex got more than his fair share of our "couple friends," and my best friend in Philly recently had her first child and disappeared into diapers, late-night feedings, and Mommy and Me outings.

I backed out of the fridge. "This is so kind of you."

Cleo shrugged. "This house is old and has some issues. But I love living here, and I hope you like it too."

"Well, I do like a house with history." I thought of my antique piecrust table and the three boxes of LPs from the

'70s that I had yet to unpack. "Actually, anything with history."

"That fits. You're the new director of the local history museum, right?"

I paused. "Starting Monday. How did you know?"

"The landlord's a cousin of mine. He told me."

I led her into the living room, gestured to the couch, and opened the pizza box. "Would you like a slice?"

"I already had dinner at my parents', but maybe one." She tipped her head toward the wine bottle. "Shall I open that? It's a screw top."

"After today, a little wine sounds wonderful." I slid a slice of pizza onto a napkin, opened my salad container, and drizzled on the dressing.

Cleo poured some wine in each cup, handed one to me, and sat down, then bounced back up to take a piece of pizza.

She struck me as one of those high-energy people who talked fast, worked fast, and probably could eat an extra slice of pizza anytime she wanted without gaining an ounce. She was taller than me, maybe five feet, eight inches to my five feet, five inches, and slimmer. Her blond hair was cut in a pixie with long bangs, far more stylish than the shoulder-length bob I'd worn for years. She had skin almost as light as mine, although I'd probably win out in a contest to see who got sunburned the fastest. Her oversized glasses gave her a dramatic air, and even in tan capris, tennis shoes, and a cobalt blue T-shirt, she somehow looked pulled together.

"This is much more fun than unpacking." I raised my cup.

"I'm glad we have a chance to get to know each other." She touched her cup to mine as if to say cheers and took a quick sip. "So, tell me about yourself."

I settled farther back into the corner of the couch. "Well, I'm thirty-two, divorced, born in Columbus, Ohio, and until three days ago, I lived in Philly."

"And your mother was Adelaide Dorsett before she married, right?"

"She was." I tried to look nonchalant, but Cleo must have noticed my surprise.

"You'll be shocked how much people know about you, living in a small town. I used to hate it, but after a while, I got used to it. And you, of course, being related to Elsie, are practically royalty."

Elsie Dorsett, my great-great grandmother and a former mayor of Dogwood Springs, had instigated many of the changes that made the town so attractive to tourists. Apparently, that ancestry was still a big deal. Not quite big enough to be royalty, though.

"I'll have to unpack my crown." I chuckled, snagged another napkin, and wiped my fingers. "So, what about you?"

"I run a hair salon, creatively named Cleo's." She grinned. "I'm thirty, I've never been married, and I've lived here all my life except for eight years in my late teens and early twenties when I studied hair design and worked at a salon in New York City."

Ahh, she was a hair stylist. That explained why her honey-gold hair had perfect highlights and lowlights, as opposed to my own hair, which was plain dark brown. "I have to say, I'm surprised you moved back."

"So were a lot of other people." Cleo rolled her eyes.

"And what about your dog? What's its name?"

Cleo looked over at the golden retriever, lying contentedly in front of the fireplace. "Oh, that's Bella. She's not mine. She belonged to the man who used to live in this apartment, Don Felding. He was quite elderly and passed away."

A dull ache formed in the back of my throat. No wonder the dog had wandered through my apartment. She was probably searching for her former owner. "Poor Bella."

"I know." Cleo's face clouded. "She's the sweetest dog ever. I should have told you who she was before you let her in. It feels so natural to have her here that I didn't think of it at first. She lives with Don's daughter, Melinda, in a house that's maybe eight blocks away." Cleo pointed the direction of my bedroom, which I thought was south. "She works at a hospital up in Jefferson City, an hour away."

I called the dog over, found a number on the tag attached to her collar, and grabbed my cell phone. "I'll let Melinda know Bella's here." After a brief conversation, I hung up. "She says she'll be by to get her in a couple of hours once her shift is over and she makes the drive home."

Bella looked up at me.

I ran a hand over the soft fur between her ears. She was a beautiful dog, well behaved and gentle, and she seemed to bask in my attention. If she was going to be here a while, the least I could do was offer her some water.

I opened a box marked "Dishes," unwrapped a blue-flowered serving bowl, and filled it with water from the kitchen tap.

Bella took a long drink, then returned to the fireplace and laid down with a soft snuffle.

"I have a feeling," Cleo said as I returned to the couch, "that Bella really misses Don."

"I bet. Change is hard." I should know. Getting divorced and losing my job were hard enough, and now I'd moved. And as far as prestige went, my new position in Dogwood Springs was a cliff-drop down from my role at the Henry C. Branch House.

Plus, small-town life was bound to be different, possibly a bit dull. I was determined to do my best, though, to adjust.

Cleo and I visited a while longer and, between us, ate half the pizza. Not long after she went upstairs, Melinda Felding arrived, apologized profusely, explained that her backyard gate might not have been latched properly, and called to Bella.

The big dog stopped to rub her head against my leg, looked up at me with doleful eyes, and followed Melinda to her car.

I waved and went back inside, my heart heavy.

Probably exhaustion.

I made up my bed, took a hot shower, and was asleep within five minutes.

The next day arrived bright and sunny, and as soon as I got dressed, I stepped out onto the concrete front porch of the house. The humidity had yet to arrive, the sky was a vivid blue, and the trees on Elm Street—which were actually mostly maples—were a rich green. I watched a robin yank a worm out of the front yard and then went back inside.

I dawdled over breakfast, working a crossword puzzle on my phone, and then unpacked the kitchen. A little before twelve, I ate a peanut butter sandwich and moved on to unboxing my clothes. I laid out a black skirt, black flats, and my favorite green shirt, the one that was the exact color of my eyes, to wear the next day, my first day at the museum.

By three that afternoon, I'd made good progress unpacking my clothes. I decided to reward my efforts with a drive around Dogwood Springs.

I went out my kitchen door, passed the outside metal stairs that led up to Cleo's back door and little deck, and crossed the yard to the separate double garage.

I carefully backed out, grateful I didn't drive a larger car, turned around, and headed out the gravel drive between numbers 406 and 408 South Elm Street, turning right on Elm.

Half a block later, I made a left onto Fourth and took it to Main Street, the heart of downtown. I'd been here before, both when I was a child visiting my grandparents and when I came into town for the interview, but I looked at things a lot more closely now that Dogwood Springs was my new home.

My parents still lived in Columbus, Ohio, where I'd grown up, but Mom thought my move to her hometown was the smartest thing I'd done in years. According to her, Dogwood Springs was a gem among small towns. I had to admit she was probably right.

Downtown had been pretty in April when I came for my interview. It was even prettier now, in June, with the maples that lined both sides of Main Street fully leafed out. The huge baskets that hung from each antique-style light post had held pansies in April but were now heavily weighed down with pink and purple and white petunias. And as I'd noticed before, there were upscale restaurants, a large library, a candy shop, a bookstore, a gift shop, a bakery, and a store called "It Always Fits," which had a window display of scarves, purses, and jewelry. All of this and more within walking distance of my very reasonably priced apartment. I didn't want to be disloyal to Philadelphia, but Dogwood Springs seemed really nice.

At four o'clock on a Sunday afternoon in June, the side-walks along Main Street were filled with shoppers, including a man eating a big piece of fudge, a girl of about ten walking a pair of small, fluffy white dogs, and four women in matching hot pink T-shirts that said "Eat, Shop, Sleep. Repeat."

The history museum, which was a large, white, two-story Greek Revival, sat at the far edge of the business district, two doors down from the bookstore. What could be nicer? I could take a sandwich for lunch some days, eat it quickly, and then pop over and find a new book. Maybe this move would turn out to be all right.

I drove slowly past the museum, giving myself a pep talk aloud about the new job, and followed Main Street out of the downtown area until it became a two-lane highway.

After a mile or so, I turned onto Red Barn Road and drove out toward Ashlington, my mother's family home. The road wound past corn and wheat fields and through woods of oak and cedar. Excitement bubbled in my chest as I crossed Cedar Creek. I might be all grown up, but part of me was still five years old, eager to celebrate Christmas or the Fourth of July surrounded by my grandparents, aunts and uncles, and cousins at Ashlington.

As I got closer, I slowed. Did I really want to see the house? What if it was too depressing? What if the owners came outside while I was driving by? I wasn't sure I wanted to explain the pull the house and land had on me.

But maybe they would understand. Maybe they had felt it too. Maybe that's why they bought the place.

I rounded the last curve, and a bittersweet ache pinched the base of my throat. There it was.

Ashlington.

The pale peach house sat atop a ridge, and beyond its wide backyard, the rolling Ozark hills spread out, fields alternating with forest in a glorious green patchwork. As for the house itself, Ashlington was two-and-a-half stories of Victorian architecture at its finest. A wide front porch arced out to form a rounded entryway, and a matching balcony above provided a private porch that had been my grand-mother's breakfast spot. The roofline sported twin chimneys, gingerbread details, and—my favorite feature—a turret. When my grandparents, Birdie and Bob Dorsett, owned the place, the turret room had been a library with walls lined with musty classics, old encyclopedias, and at least two decades of the *Farmer's Almanac*, well worn by my grandfather, an avid fisherman who trusted the predictions for good fishing days.

My ancestors who built Ashlington had made their money in lumber. When I was a young child, my grandparents had still owned the local lumberyard, been pillars of Dogwood Springs's society, and held a fabulous party each Christmas for friends, employees, and family.

By the time I was twelve, though, my grandparents were deceased, the lumberyard had closed, and the house had been passed on—half to my Aunt Gloria, the eldest, and half in smaller shares divided among my mom and her other sisters. Once my grandparents were gone, the family ties loosened. Oh, my mother and her sisters still talked on the phone every weekend, but the family had scattered across the country, and we never got together much. Finally, two years ago, after Aunt Gloria's husband died and upkeep on the house got to be too much for her, she moved to Texas to be closer to her daughter. She sold the house to some retired tech mogul, bought a new sun hat, and took up bridge. My mom, whose mouth always tightened when she spoke of the sale, said Aunt Gloria had been fleeced. In my mom's mind, Ashlington was a million-dollar mansion.

Today, as I drove closer, I spotted scaffolding at the west side of the house, where a project to repaint the trim appeared to be nearing completion. I knew what my mother had gotten after the sale, and I knew what Aunt Gloria had kept. To be honest, the tech mogul might have been kind— or perhaps not yet used to prices in rural Missouri. Ashlington, for all its charm, looked like a money pit.

I let out a sigh. Whatever its value, it still called to my heart. But even if I could have afforded it, Ashlington now belonged to someone else.

I gave a small wave, bidding farewell to the house, my happy childhood memories there, and any dreams I might have of living in the family home. Then I drove past, found a wide spot to turn around, and headed back toward town.

Toward my future.

At a supermarket on the edge of town, I loaded a cart with food and paper towels and everything else I could think of that I might need in my new home. Next door to the grocery store, I spotted a Mexican restaurant with a parking lot already crowded for dinner and a sign that said they delivered. Another win for Dogwood Springs. Mexican was my favorite. I made a mental note of the name of the place and headed home.

Ten minutes later, reveling in the lack of traffic, I pulled back into my garage.

I hefted one reusable bag in each arm and walked toward my kitchen door.

There, waiting on the welcome mat, was a rather muddy Bella.

"I'm sorry," Melinda said when I called. "This time, Bella found a way out under the fence. I don't know what I'm going to do. She's terribly lonely at my house, but I'm working a lot of double shifts. What with that and the time I spend commuting and the way Bella misses Dad, I don't know if she's ever going to like living with me." She let out an audible sigh. "I have to admit, I promised Dad I'd make sure Bella had a good home, but I never really wanted a dog."

"That is difficult." I pictured Bella, all alone for those long days. She clearly loved people, and she was such a nice dog. She'd even seemed appreciative when I wiped the mud off her paws with some of my new paper towels.

"There's a woman at the hospital who says she'll take her, but"—Melinda hesitated—"between you and me, I've met her kids, and I'm not sure they'd be nice to Bella."

I sank onto the couch.

Bella trotted over, tags jingling, and laid her head on my knee. She looked up, a plea filling her soft brown eyes.

My heart twisted. "Um, can I call you back in a few minutes?" The words slipped out before I'd thought them through.

"Oh..." Melinda sounded confused. "Sure."

I hung up and ran a hand down Bella's back. I was bound to be busy starting a new job. But I had been hoping to adopt a pet, and I knew how to care for one, since we'd had dogs, cats, and even a hamster when I was growing up.

Plus, I only lived a few blocks away from my job. I could pop home every day at lunch and let Bella out. And if I had extra work, I could bring it home in the evenings. It wasn't like an extra shift at a hospital an hour out of town. By five-thirty every day, I'd be home, free to take Bella for a walk and spend time with her.

I made a quick call to my landlord and called Melinda back. "Would you be willing to let Bella stay with me for a week, on a trial basis, to see if we get along?"

She eagerly agreed and said she'd be right over with Bella's bed, her brush, a giant bag of dog food, and a few toys.

I hung up, looked down at Bella, and drew in a deep breath. "Okay, girl, let's give this a try."

She gave me a happy doggie smile and wagged her tail.

A tingle of hope welled up inside me. Maybe, just maybe, this move might not be a mistake.

Maybe it was the fresh start I needed.

Chapter Two

ON MONDAY MORNING I got up half an hour early so I could take Bella for a walk. Sometime in the night, she'd left her bed, which I'd put in front of the fireplace, and laid down in the corner of my bedroom, bringing along her favorite toy, a well-chewed stuffed chicken. When my alarm went off, she came to the bedside and grinned at me with her tongue hanging out to one side. I petted her and told her good morning, and she waited patiently by the front door while I tossed on a T-shirt, some shorts, and my tennis shoes.

When I picked up the leash Melinda had brought over, Bella gave me a look that implied Don Felding had not wasted his time with such foolishness, but she allowed me to clip it on.

Outside, I let her take the lead, and we headed down Elm. As the numbers of the cross streets grew higher, the houses looked more expensive. I was pretty sure that, by Eighth Street, none of them were rentals.

It soon became obvious that a morning walk was not solely exercise for Bella. In the course of ten minutes, I met three of my neighbors, each of whom welcomed me to town, seemed well acquainted with Bella, and gave her plenty of love.

At Thirteenth Street, Bella looked up at me, then led me across the street and back down the sidewalk on the other side, as if she and her previous owner had followed this route many times.

Once we returned to the apartment, I showered, ate, and dressed for the day in the outfit I'd laid out, adding my mother's family pearls for confidence. I put out more dog food and water, assured Bella that I would come home at lunch to let her outside, and learned—when I casually mentioned it—that she knew the word "treat."

I left her happily munching a dog biscuit as I headed to the Dogwood Springs History Museum.

The two-story white Greek Revival had once been the home of Charles Pennington, a local man who made a fortune with an invention that had something to do with harvesting corn, a machine I needed to quickly become familiar with. The house dwarfed the lot it sat on, made Ashlington look modest, and must have seemed quite ostentatious at the time it was built. After his death, Pennington left the place to the town to be used as a history museum, along with a trust to help fund its operation as long as a display about his invention was one of the exhibits.

Of course, compared to the Henry C. Branch House, Charles Pennington's former home was a rustic cabin. And to be honest, the collection held by the Dogwood Springs History Museum was similarly unimpressive when compared with the extensive holdings the Branch family had accumulated. I let out a sigh as I went up the sidewalk to the house. No one would ever accuse me of taking this position to upgrade my resume.

I could, of course, have considered taking a job in another field. My dad had suggested I go to dental school and join the family practice where he and my brother were dentists and my mom ran the front desk.

I'd shuddered, even though I knew Dad was joking. Ever since he and Mom took my brother and me to the Smithsonian when I was in grade school and I'd seen the exhibit of the first ladies' dresses, I'd been fascinated by history.

To be sure, I had a more impressive answer I could give if someone asked why I went into public history, into museum work. I could talk about how our lives could be enriched when we knew about those who had come before us. About how museums could help visitors develop empathy for the past, the present, and each other. Really, though, it all started with those dresses. As I got older, my fascination with history expanded, but historic clothing always stayed dear to my heart.

Dentistry, not so much.

Oh, I used the top-of-the-line electric toothbrush my

parents gave me for Christmas—a new one every two years —and I religiously flossed as my father had trained me in childhood, but I had no interest in dealing with other people's teeth.

No, prestigious or not, the Dogwood Springs History Museum had a new director—me. And the museum did have some advantages that many small museums didn't. The trust allowed for a paid staff of three, and some of the town's tourist events had a strong historical component, so there were ample opportunities to promote the museum.

I straightened my shoulders and climbed the wide concrete staircase between the white columns that flanked the front door.

Inside, I inhaled the intoxicating scent of history—the slightly musty fragrance of old books and papers, the hint of mothballs that never really left some clothing, and the fresh scent of lemon furniture polish lovingly applied to antiques. Before me, a grand staircase led to the second floor. To my left and right, the former living room and dining room featured displays on the early days of the community and the role of women in its government, respectively.

I was due upstairs at nine to meet with Vivian Martin, the previous director of the museum. Before she left for her new position at a museum in Tampa, she had agreed to work an additional week to get me up to speed on the oper- ations of the museum and current potential donors, all of which I was eager to learn. I had five minutes before our meeting, though, and I couldn't resist a quick peek at the display on the role of women in Dogwood Springs's government. There, in a dark wood oval frame, was a photo of my great-great grandmother, Elsie Dorsett, who after the death of her husband had run for and been elected mayor and served in that capacity for twenty-two years.

"Libby?"

I turned.

A willowy Black woman waved from the hall. "Hi. I'm Imani Jones. We met when you were here last month."

"Nice to see you again." I walked over.

Imani was the education coordinator and gave tours to school groups, tourists, and other visitors. She was younger than me, in her late twenties, and had eyelashes any woman would envy—long, black, and completely natural looking. Her hair was braided back into a low bun, and she wore a loose, orange floral dress, a lightweight white sweater, and darling brown leather sandals.

"Welcome to the museum." She smiled and spread her arms wide, a gesture that looked like something she used when she met a tour group.

"Thanks."

A man with gray hair and a ruddy complexion, who I recognized as the museum's curator, approached from the back of the first floor. "Rodney Grant." He held out a hand. "Glad you're here."

I shook his hand, assured him I remembered him from my interview, and congratulated him on a recent acquisition Vivian had mentioned. "I guess I better head on up." I started toward the stairs. "I'm supposed to meet Vivian and begin learning the ropes."

"I'll walk up with you and show you where her office is." Imani gestured for me to lead the way up the wide, walnut stairs with an ornately carved railing. At the top, she turned toward the front of the house, the heels of her sandals making soft *clunks* on the carpet.

Rodney followed us up but turned the other way at the top of the stairs.

Like the first floor, the second had wide, ornate crown molding and baseboards. The walls were a creamy white, lined with early photos of the town, and the hardwood floor was covered with a burgundy runner. We made a slight jog to the right, and Imani stopped at a closed door. "Maybe Vivian overslept. She almost always has her door open."

Imani knocked, and the door swung wide.

"Vivian?" Imani took a half step into the room. "Libby's here to—" She let out a high-pitched scream and rushed into the room.

My stomach tensed. Cautiously, I went in.

Sunbeams filtered through the dark wooden blinds, supplementing the light from the overhead fixture and illuminating dust motes that hung in the air, the luster of the large mahogany desk...

And Vivian's body, slumped in the chair behind it.

Her champagne-blond hair was perfectly styled, her head tipped to one side, and her black-and-white paisley blouse was stained with a blotch of dark red blood.

Imani placed two fingers against Vivian's neck. "I don't feel any pulse, but my hand is shaking so much that I'm not sure."

"Call 911." My stomach grew even tighter, but I forced myself to move closer. "I'll... I'll try."

I pressed my fingers against Vivian's throat but felt nothing except the fact that her skin was still warm. I held a finger right under her nose. Surely, if she was alive, I would feel her breath.

Nothing.

I shook my head at Imani, who now stood in the doorway, phone to her ear.

"We need the police. Vivian Martin is dead," she said into the phone. "I think maybe somebody shot her."

There was no *maybe* about it.

I was far more likely to watch a gentle British mystery on PBS than any variation of *CSI*, but even I could recognize a gunshot wound.

I scanned the area around Vivian, and my pulse sped. There was no gun in her hand, no gun on the floor, no gun anywhere in the room.

Someone had killed her and taken the weapon with them.

And that someone could still be in the building.

My mouth went dry, and I glanced into the hall.

Imani had stepped out of my line of sight to talk to the 911 operator.

Maybe I was paranoid, but I wasn't going out there without some kind of weapon. But what could I find in Vivian's office? A stapler? A book?

The sun slid up past another slat in the window blinds and glinted off a small, bronze-colored statue of Harry S

Truman on the corner of Vivian's desk. It was only about ten inches tall, but the bust—of the only US president who hailed from Missouri—looked like a weapon to me. I tested its weight, then slipped it into the huge shoulder bag I used as a briefcase. I walked out of the room, jogged back to the left, and found Imani in the main hall.

"Yes, I'm still on the line," Imani said into the phone.

Rodney stood beside her, his posture rigid.

Imani pointed at a woman rushing up the stairs. Fifty-ish, she had chin-length, tousled light brown hair and wore a teal pantsuit and low heels. "Alice VanMeter," Imani mouthed.

I nodded. Alice was the president of the museum's board of directors and, according to what Vivian said when I interviewed, the best volunteer the organization had. I'd met Alice, along with most of the rest of the board, at my interview, and she'd called to offer me the job.

"What's going on? Imani looks scared to death." Alice reached the top of the stairs and started toward us.

"Stop." I held out a hand and hurried toward her. No need for anyone else to see the body. "Something horrible has happened to Vivian, and we're waiting for the police."

"The police?" Alice's brown eyes widened.

There was no easy way to say this. "Vivian's dead. We think she's been shot."

Alice took a step back. "Goodness." She glanced toward Vivian's office. "In there?"

"I'm afraid so."

Her lips thinned. "I see," she said calmly. This woman was clearly good in a crisis.

Imani angled the phone away from her mouth. "The 911 operator says it will be a few minutes before anyone gets here. There was a three-car accident down by the university."

Which meant we were alone in the building. Possibly with a killer. "Is anyone else here?"

"Not that I know of," Imani said. "We don't usually unlock the front door this early. I only unlocked it because we were expecting you."

I peered up and down the hall. "Does anyone else have a key?"

Rodney angled his head toward Imani. "Vivian, us, everyone on the board."

"Okay," I said. "Well, I think we need to stick together and get out of here."

Rodney and Alice nodded. They'd already come to the same conclusion I had.

Imani stiffened as the implication sank in. "Oh, um, yeah." She moved closer to Rodney, slightly wobbly on her heels.

Footsteps echoed up the stairwell, and the three of us froze. I slipped a hand into my shoulder bag and frantically dug around until my fingers closed on the head of Harry S Truman. I pulled the bust from my bag, raised it over my head, and moved closer to the others. The four of us formed a wall with our backs to Vivian's office.

"Whoa. What's going on here?" A man in his forties

came to the top of the stairs and jerked his head to peer at us one by one, ending with me.

I slid the statue back into my bag but kept my hand on it. "There's been an ... an incident." Who was this guy? Surely, I'd remember him if I'd met him before. He reminded me of a skinny white rabbit in a business suit. Pale skin, pale strawberry-blond hair, and washed-out blue eyes. "I'm Libby Ballard, the new museum director. Is there a reason you're in the building before it's open?"

"I'm Dwight Bower, board treasurer. I wasn't at your interview. Is Vivian around? I need her signature."

"No." I released my grip on the statue. "And it's going to be rather hard to get her to sign anything."

"Oh." His forehead bunched up. "Are you on the account yet?"

"Vivian's dead," Imani blurted out.

Dwight's mouth fell open. "What happened?"

"I'd say she was shot," Imani said.

"Wow." Dwight ran a hand over his chest.

Outside, the wail of sirens began softly, then grew louder. "I imagine that's the police." I pointed toward the stairs. "We should go to the front door."

One by one, the others somberly filed down the wide, wooden staircase toward the entryway. I took up the rear, mind racing.

I didn't really know Vivian. I met her at the interview, and we'd spoken on the phone. She seemed eager to begin her new job in Florida and grateful to be passing off her work to me.

In all our interactions, she had seemed professional. Not particularly friendly, but professional.

But maybe that lack of warmth wasn't only with me. Maybe she'd been cold with everyone.

Because no one—not Imani or Rodney, who worked with Vivian every day, not Dwight, or even Alice—had expressed any sorrow that she was gone.

Chapter Three

THREE POLICE OFFICERS came through the front door of the museum.

Talking over each other, Rodney, Imani, Alice, Dwight, and I tried to explain what had happened.

The oldest officer, who was short and heavyset with a salt-and-pepper buzz cut, seemed to take it all in, then held up a hand to stop us. He asked if any of us had been harmed. We said we were fine, and he ordered the two younger officers to search the building.

They headed up the staircase, and he hurried us outside.

"I'm Detective John Harper." He pointed to a metal bench that sat near the sidewalk in front of the house next to the museum. "Let's go over there to talk."

Alice led the way. Dwight, Rodney, Imani, and I followed in a clump, as if afraid to be separated from each other. The detective brought up the rear.

As we drew closer to the bench next door, I read the gold

script on the glass front door, which identified it as an appraiser's office. The building was partly hidden behind trees, and I'd thought it was a private home.

Imani sank onto the bench, let out a shaky sigh, and hunched forward, head in her hands.

Harper touched her arm. "Are you sure you're all right?"

She looked back up. "I am. It was just ... just..."

Alice sat beside her and patted her shoulder. "It's okay, Imani. You're safe."

The detective nodded and turned to me. His thick eyebrows, several shades darker than his graying buzz cut, drew together. "I need your name and address, ma'am."

"Libby, um, Elizabeth Ballard, 406 South Elm Street. I'm the new director of the museum. It's my first day. Imani was taking me up to meet with Vivian when we found the body."

I thought he might recognize my name, but he simply wrote down my information.

Perhaps the owner of the bed and breakfast hadn't mentioned me when she took the evidence of the burglary I'd helped solve back in April to the police.

Harper looked up from his notepad at me. "Was the museum open?"

"No, it doesn't open until ten." I glanced at Imani for confirmation.

Imani nodded.

The detective turned to Rodney. "I know you work at the museum too, but I don't know what your job is."

"Curator." Rodney provided his address and gestured to the bench. "Libby, would you like to sit down?"

I shook my head, and Rodney joined Imani and Alice on the bench. He rubbed his right knee and let out a heavy sigh. "Sorry. My knee replacement can't come a day too soon."

Alice patted his shoulder.

Harper looked at Dwight. "You don't work at the museum. Why were you there before it opened?"

"I needed someone—either Vivian or Libby—to cosign a check. I'm the treasurer. I'm a CPA." He directed the last comment at me, as if it was for my benefit.

I gave what I hoped was a believable smile. Having a CPA on the board was an enormous asset for a small museum. I should be grateful for his help. The timing of his visit to the museum, though, made him a prime suspect in my mind, and there was something about him that made me uneasy.

At least I thought it was him.

Maybe it was the whole situation.

After all, Alice and Imani had accepted Dwight's explanation of why he was in the building, and neither one seemed frightened of him.

Unable to help myself, I edged slightly away from him, closer to Alice.

The officer took down Dwight's address and turned to Alice. "I assume you're on the board as well?"

"I am."

Harper took her address. Then he turned to Imani, who

he also seemed to know. He made sure he had the correct spelling of her name, asked what she did at the museum, and wrote down her address.

His radio squawked, and he said something into it that I didn't quite catch.

"There's no one in the museum," Harper told us. "Let's go inside. One of my officers says there's a conference room."

"Yes," Alice said. "In the back. It's the original kitchen."

"Fine. I'll speak with each of you individually there."

The detective let us in the building, told us not to touch anything, and left us sitting on the upholstered benches in the entry hall with one of the younger officers to guard us. "Wait here quietly, please, and don't discuss what has happened." He tipped his head toward one of the young officers. "If you need anything, ask Officer Davis. Miss Jones, if you'll come with me."

Imani, who had been sitting closest to the front door, rose but made no move toward the detective.

"I'm sure you'll be fine." Alice stood and, for the briefest of seconds, touched a hand to Imani's back like a mom urging on a child. "Just explain what happened."

"Officer Tate, you're with me." The detective glanced at the other young officer and motioned for Imani to go ahead.

She looked back at Alice, then left the room with Detective Harper and Officer Tate.

Officer Davis leaned back, arms crossed over his chest, and watched us intently. Based on how young he looked, I'd guess this was his first murder investigation and he was eager for one of us to slip up, confess that we'd killed Vivian, and allow him to solve the case.

Instead, Alice, Rodney, Dwight, and I sat silently.

Dwight picked at his cuticles, then asked if he could use his phone to let his office know he'd be late. The officer agreed. I watched as Dwight sent a text, opened an app, and began reading.

Alice sat calmly, gaze distant, as if she were thinking of things she planned to do after the police released us.

Rodney picked up a newspaper from the end of the bench, but I didn't think he was really reading it. No one could look at the front page that long.

For a moment, I contemplated the fact that there had been a burglary at the B & B when I came to town for my interview, then a murder on my first day of work. Odd, but clearly, just a strange coincidence. After all, there was a lot more crime in Philadelphia than in a small town like Dogwood Springs.

But crime in a museum came with its own set of complications. Many artifacts were one of a kind. Responsibility for the collection and discovery of a dead body was a lot to deal with on my first day.

I pulled a small notepad from my bag and wrote down details of what I had seen in Vivian's office. When it was my turn to talk to the detective, I wanted to give him all the information I could. The sooner he solved this case, the better.

Alice was interviewed next, followed by Dwight. When it was Rodney's turn, he slowly got to his feet. As he walked away, I heard him say how vital it was that the police not get fingerprint powder on the artifacts and that they allow him to check to make sure nothing had been stolen. I nodded gratefully. I'd be reiterating those exact same points.

Finally, it was my turn to be interviewed.

Officer Tate came to the entry hall and led me to the conference room. Unlike the display rooms, it had been updated. It had a modern sink, a minifridge, and a coffee station along one wall, but the remodel looked like a low-budget job. The vinyl floor, a pattern designed to look like cream tiles with mauve grout, had probably been laid in the 1980s.

Detective Harper sat at a long wooden table in the middle of the room. Officer Tate gestured for me to sit across from the detective. Tate sat beside the detective and took out a notepad.

The detective looked over at me. "Miss Ballard, Rodney has volunteered to go through the museum to see if anything was stolen. Is that all right with you?"

"That would be wonderful. I don't really know the collection yet. And if it's at all possible, could you—"

"Be careful with the fingerprint powder?"

I nodded.

"Rodney already made that point about six times. We do have to collect evidence, but we'll be as careful as we can."

I expressed my gratitude, then gave my statement, answering each question as best I could, describing when I arrived, who I saw, and what I noticed about the crime scene.

"Had you met Ms. Martin before today?"

"Yes, I met Vivian when I interviewed for the job in April."

Harper made a note on his pad.

"I also talked with her on the phone a few times. She seemed eager to make sure I had all the information necessary to take over her position. That's why she was here today. She was going to spend the week introducing me to potential donors and discussing a big grant proposal she planned to submit."

He nodded. "And when you found the body, Miss Jones went into Vivian's office first?"

"Yes." I thought for a moment. "She knocked, called out 'Libby's here,' as the door swung open, and started to go in. Then she screamed and rushed into the room."

He made another note. "And she touched the body?"

"Yes, we both did, trying to see if Vivian was still alive."

"You said Miss Jones was in the room before you were?"

"Yes."

"Were you with her the entire time after you found the body until I arrived?"

I thought for a moment. "No. She stepped out into the hall and around the corner. I think the sight of the body—" I made a helpless gesture with my hands.

"So, she could have removed evidence from the scene and hidden it elsewhere on the second floor."

"I guess," I said slowly. "She couldn't have gone very far. I joined her in the hall pretty quickly." I leaned forward. "I really don't think Imani was the killer. She looked too shocked when we found the body."

Harper gave me a pained look, as if he thought I was naïve. "We'll figure this out, Miss Ballard. We have to consider all possibilities at this point." He leaned back in his chair. "I think that's all my questions for now. We'll type up your statement, and you'll need to come down to the station to sign it after lunch tomorrow. And I need to ask you to stay in Dogwood Springs until this is wrapped up."

I felt my shoulders stiffen. "Am I a suspect?"

"It's purely routine. I may need to ask you more questions."

I exhaled.

He rose and walked back with me to the entry hall, where I remembered Rodney's sore knee and offered to help him with the inventory.

Rodney said he thought he'd be more efficient alone, so I made sure he had my number. He promised to provide the police with a key and to call as soon as he finished checking the exhibits.

Detective Harper cleared his throat. "Rodney, Officer Tate will go through the museum with you. Dwight, Alice, Libby, you all are free to go. Miss Jones, I'd like you to come down to the station. We have a few more questions for you."

Imani gulped, and her eyes widened.

The detective turned to me. "Miss Ballard, the museum needs to remain closed until we finish gathering evidence. I will call you when we're done. I apologize in advance for the fact that it may take a few days. We were short-staffed before, and today, half the force is out with food poisoning from a birthday party they attended last night. For now, let me walk out with you."

Outside, Officer Davis stood beside the front door of the museum, and Detective Harper put Imani in the back of a police car.

"Holy smoke," Dwight said. "They think she did it."

"Imani is a nice girl." Alice's mouth tightened. "I can't believe she's capable of murder."

Dwight gave her a sideways glance. "You do remember the last board meeting, don't you?"

"Humph." Alice looked down her nose at him. "I still don't believe she's a killer."

"What happened at the last board meeting?" I asked.

Dwight leaned toward me.

Something about him still made me uneasy. I had to force myself not to back away.

He took a step even closer. "Vivian told us that, unless you had strong objections, in her last duty as director, she was going to fire Imani. Apparently, Imani messed up a huge email campaign that Vivian had been counting on to bring in significant donations."

"Oh." There was a lot going on here that I was totally clueless about.

Dwight's phone rang. He answered, mumbled something into the phone, and hung up. "I should get to my office."

Alice checked her watch. "And I've got to pick up my

grandsons." She laid a hand on my shoulder. "Libby, are you okay on your own?"

"I am." Even if I felt odd having touched the body of someone who'd been murdered. "I think I'll head home and take a shower, try to relax a bit."

"That sounds like a good plan." Alice patted my shoulder, then she and Dwight headed toward the parking lot behind the museum.

I walked as far as the bookstore. Then I glanced back at the officer guarding the front door of the museum and headed home.

What a day.

My new job at the Dogwood Springs History Museum was not starting off the way I had hoped.

The former director was dead, the museum had been temporarily closed, and one of my staff members was suspected of murder.

Bella greeted me at the front door, tail wagging at top speed. Tears sprang to my eyes, and I knelt and pulled her close, soaking up the connection as scenes from the day swirled in my head like dandelion fluff picked up by the wind. I walked to the kitchen, pulled the heavy Truman bust from my purse, and put it on the counter, then let Bella outside. I sat on the back steps and called my dad at work, luckily catching him between patients.

I gave him an abbreviated version of the day, which he

agreed to pass along to my mom with repeated assurances that I was not in any danger. I knew if I called her with the shock still this raw, she'd immediately pick up on my stress, and it would cycle in some weird feedback loop, leaving me even more upset. Dad, on the other hand, told me the police would catch the killer and the new job would work out fine.

I got off the phone, took a shower, and fixed Bella and myself some lunch. After lunch, I brushed her coat as I told her all the details of the day.

Finally, after I had cut out a small mat of fur on one of her hind legs and brushed the rest until it gleamed, I gave her a pat on the head. "We'll have to do this several times a week, girl, to keep your coat in good condition."

She laid her head on my knee as if to say she was more than willing. Then she looked up at me with such affection that it made my heart ache. In her eyes, I felt perfect, loved beyond measure. My ex-husband had once loved me like that, had once made me feel like I was the most important person in the world.

Trusting him, believing him, building a life with him ... hadn't turned out so well.

I gave Bella a big hug and kissed the top of her head. "I'm so glad you're in my life now, girl."

I don't know if she somehow sensed that I was upset, but she stuck right at my side as we walked down Elm Street, turned at Thirteenth Street, and returned home. And the rest of the afternoon, she stayed extra close. At one point, she even brought over her stuffed chicken and dropped it by my feet. I didn't find it quite as comforting as she obviously meant it to be, but I appreciated the gesture. She really was an incredible sweetie.

Eventually, her presence made me feel a little more normal.

More normal, but still shell-shocked.

The Internet was not yet on in my new apartment, but after our walk, I connected to a streaming service on my phone and binge-watched the happiest show I could think of, a sitcom from the eighties. I ordered chicken tacos delivered for dinner and had some of my emergency shortbread for dessert. If ever there was an event that called for the soothing combination of butter and sugar, finding a dead body was it. Just after I finished eating, Rodney called and told me that, to the best of his knowledge, nothing had been stolen from the museum. I thanked him profusely and was starting another episode of the sitcom when someone knocked at my door.

I paused the show on my phone, ran my fingers through my hair, and walked to the door, Bella at my heels.

Cleo peered through the narrow window beside the door that led from the entryway to my apartment. When I opened the door, she enveloped me in a hug. "I'm so glad you're okay. I heard someone was shot at the museum today."

"It was Vivian, the former director," I said.

Cleo inhaled and gripped the collar of her bright purple shirt. "I know her. She was one of my clients. She came in for the exact same cut and color every month. Never an update, no matter how hard I tried to convince her." Cleo shook her head. "What a horrible thing to have happen on your first day."

"It was. Especially since we found her body in what will be my office."

Cleo's eyes widened. "Really? *You* found the body? That's even worse."

"Imani Jones, the member services coordinator, and me." I led Cleo into the living room and sat on one end of the couch, gesturing to the other.

She sat, leaned forward, and listened intently as I explained what all had happened.

"I don't really know what to think." How should I say this? "But I have a feeling Detective Harper's on the wrong track. He suspects Imani, and she was totally shocked when we found Vivian."

Cleo let out a sigh. "The police chief, Detective Harper's brother, Wes Harper, had a heart attack a few weeks ago and is still at home recovering. Sue Ann, the dispatcher—she's another one of my regulars—says the police were already short-staffed before Wes's heart attack. Detective Harper has been pulled into administrative stuff and still has to do his own job." She paused for a quick breath. "Sue Ann says he's overwhelmed."

Tension built in my chest. "I really don't think Imani did it. And the killer needs to be caught and put in jail." Justice, which I'd never given a great deal of thought to in the past, meant a lot more to me after the way I'd been unfairly treated by my ex.

"Yeah. You don't want whoever did this out on the loose,

Libby. They might come back to the museum. If it was me, I'd be wondering if I even wanted the job."

My stomach sank. "I can't really imagine feeling safe there."

As if she'd heard the stress in my voice, Bella came over and laid her head on my knee. I patted the silky fur between her ears.

I had absolutely no desire to sit in my office at the Dogwood Springs History Museum, waiting for someone to sneak in and kill me too.

And I couldn't imagine anyone wanting to visit the museum in the current situation either. Which meant revenue would plummet, and donors would keep their checkbooks closed. All of which would lead to my failure as director. I sank back against the couch. It was bad enough losing my position at the Henry C. Branch House. If I was let go from the Dogwood Springs History Museum, I'd never find another job at a museum. Talk about a no-win situation.

"Seriously," Cleo said. "Do you want to go back to your old job?"

An interesting question. Would I rather work with my ex or around a murderer? My ex-husband won but only by a hair. "Sadly, that's not an option. The market for museum jobs isn't great. I was lucky to get this position."

And I needed it to work out. The past few months without a job had taken a toll on my finances. At this point, I had three options for covering my living expenses. I could make this job work. I could sell my pearls, but I wasn't sure they were worth that much. Or I could ask my parents for money, which I really didn't want to do. Oh, they were fairly well off, and they'd be happy to help. But except for a couple small scholarships, my parents had paid for my undergrad at Ohio University, and they'd helped out when I got my master's. I didn't want to go back to being dependent on them. I wanted to stand on my own two feet.

But I wasn't certain Detective Harper would ever find the killer if he was that overworked, especially with the way he'd targeted Imani. And if the police weren't going to solve the crime...

"Maybe there's another option." I sat up taller.

Was I crazy to even consider it? Like any historian, I was good at putting puzzle pieces together. And I instinctively approached things logically. Look at how I'd figured out who was behind that burglary at the bed and breakfast.

Plus, I was certainly highly motivated. If I was going to make a success of this new job, I needed the museum to be open and cleared of any link to a crime.

But I also had another reason for wanting to solve this case. Although I'd never admitted it out loud, I'd felt like a victim in Philadelphia. A victim of my husband's infidelity. A victim of the divorce. A victim of how my ex had manipulated our boss at the museum into eliminating my position.

This move was all about change, about taking charge of my own life and beginning a new, better chapter. I was not going to let myself—and my future in Dogwood Springs—be an indirect victim of this crime.

I raised my chin and looked over at Cleo. "I'd need information about possible suspects, but you're a hairdresser. Don't you know all the secrets in town?"

"Some of them, yes. But if you're saying what I think you're saying, that you want to try to figure this out on your own…" She raised her eyebrows.

"I am."

She dipped her chin and gave me a look that said she was impressed. "Then you need info from someone connected to the museum. Someone you can trust." Cleo tapped her lips with one finger. "Doesn't Alice VanMeter volunteer at the museum?"

"She does. She was there this morning, in fact. And she's the president of the board, the person who hired me."

"You can trust her."

"Are you sure?"

"Yep. She's smart. She knows everyone. And she was my Sunday school teacher in high school."

"Do you think she'd help me?"

"Oh, yeah. She loves that museum. In fact, she loves everything about this town."

I thought back to how I'd instinctively moved away from Dwight and toward Alice. "Okay. I'll call her and see if she can meet me tomorrow to talk. The museum is closed until the police finish collecting evidence."

Cleo nodded. "Can we meet early? I have to open the salon at ten."

"You want to join us?"

"Of course I do. Alice will be great for information, but I've watched TV. You don't want to go into dangerous situations alone. If you go out hunting for clues, it'll be better if I go with you, instead of Alice."

"Because…"

"Because I lived in some pretty bad neighborhoods in New York. I've taken a lot of self-defense classes." She raised her arms as if she were about to give an attacker a karate chop.

"Wow. Thanks." A bubble of hope welled up inside me. I wasn't trapped in a no-win situation. This wasn't my divorce all over again. I had a plan. And I had Cleo to help me, someone who was turning out to be a real friend. Surely, we could figure out who killed Vivian. "I've got Alice's number. Is there a good place we could meet for breakfast to talk?"

"The Dogwood Café on Main Street. Their pancakes are to die for."

I shot her a look. "To *die* for? Probably not the best endorsement, given the situation. But I ate dinner there when I came for my interview, and it was delicious. I'll see if Alice can meet us. Maybe nine?"

Cleo agreed, and Alice did as well when I called.

I hung up and tried to hold back a yawn. "Sorry. I think the day has caught up with me."

Cleo gave me another hug, reminded me that she was right upstairs if I needed her, and headed to her apartment.

I got ready for bed, determined that tomorrow I would find the killer.

Chapter Four

"ARE you sure Bella can come with us?" I sat down on my couch the next morning to put on my tennis shoes.

"You bet." Cleo stood near the door of my apartment, petting Bella. "I see dogs in the outside seating area at the café all the time."

I grabbed my purse, clipped on Bella's leash, and the three of us walked downtown.

The Dogwood Café sat in the heart of Main Street, situated about ten feet farther back from the street than the neighboring shops. A low metal fence enclosed the seating area out front, which was filled with green metal tables and chairs. Cleo snagged a table in the corner as a group was leaving.

"This will be perfect." She pointed to a triangular space between the table and the fence. "This spot in the corner is perfect for Bella, and we need room for four. My nephew is joining us."

"Your nephew?"

"Zeke. My sister-in-law's dropping him off on her way to work. He's coming to fix the salon's computer today."

"Maybe I should let you and Zeke get your own table." I hesitated. I didn't want to sit down if we might need two smaller tables. "This conversation with Alice could be awkward. Having another person there might make it even harder."

Cleo brushed away my concerns with a wave of her hand. "Zeke won't be part of the conversation, I promise you. He'll sit there with his earbuds in, inhaling the biggest plate of pancakes the café serves, playing with his phone."

I glanced over at her. "How old is Zeke?"

"Fifteen."

"And you're going to let him fix the computer at your salon?"

"Let him? I *begged* him to fix it. He's way better with that stuff than anyone else I know. And all it will cost me is breakfast and three hours of taking him out for driving practice. He's eager to get his license."

"Oh." Maybe my worries were unfounded. It sounded as if Zeke wasn't going to be listening to our conversation.

After Bella got plenty of love from people at the next table, I slipped her a dog biscuit. She happily settled down in the shady corner by the fence.

A server dropped off menus and water for four, and I perused the options. Cleo gave her menu a single pat but didn't open it.

A couple minutes later, she stood and waved.

A lanky boy with a long, dark ponytail approached, hauling a huge backpack. He wore black Converse tennis shoes, baggy shorts, and a T-shirt advertising something I thought was a video game. He sat by Cleo, across from me.

Cleo elbowed him, introduced us, and when Zeke remained silent, glared at him and said loudly, "Nice to meet you."

Zeke echoed the greeting, petted Bella, and pulled his phone and earbuds from his pocket. Then he slumped down in his chair and disappeared into his phone.

"Libby?"

I turned. Alice had walked up behind me, and I hadn't even noticed. "I'm so sorry. Please, join us."

"Nice to see you," she said to Cleo.

I scrambled for an explanation. "Cleo's here for—"

"Moral support," Cleo put in. "And Zeke's here for the pancakes." She gestured to her nephew, who ignored her.

"Sorry I'm a little late." Alice ran a hand down her navy print blouse and navy dress pants. "I was picking up some fertilizer at the garden center, and they had a new cashier who was a little lost. Anyway, I'm so glad you invited me to join you." She grimaced. "I can't believe John Harper suspects Imani."

I shook my head. "I can't either."

"What you must think of Dogwood Springs." Alice sat. "The board was so thrilled that you took the director's position. We want it to be a wonderful experience for you. Not" —she made an awkward gesture with her hands—"this."

"Thank you." I wanted that too, but ... how should I

word this? I'd only been in town three days. It was a little soon to start criticizing the locals. "I, um, I thought if we put our heads together and maybe I asked around a bit, we might come up with some information that could help Detective Harper find the real killer."

"I think the police are really short-staffed, especially since the chief had that heart attack," Cleo said.

Alice nodded. "I've heard that. And I appreciate that you want this solved, Libby, and that you want to clear Imani's name. But I'd hate for you to put yourself in danger."

I assured her I would be very careful. "I'm not going to meet anyone in a dark alley or anything. And the minute I learn anything useful, I'll take it to the police."

Alice didn't seem fully comfortable, but she agreed that it was better than the alternative. "I do hate the idea of sitting around, waiting for something else bad to happen."

A woman after my own heart.

Our server returned and poured coffee for Alice and Cleo. She raised the pot toward my mug, but I held a hand over it.

Zeke pulled out his earbuds, and the server took our orders, including hot tea for me and a large soda for Zeke.

A second later, the earbuds were back in, and he was absorbed in his phone.

"So, I guess I'll plunge in." I pulled my notepad from my bag and looked at Alice. "My first question is about Vivian herself. How come"—there was no way to say this nicely— "no one seemed sorry she was dead?"

"I can answer that." Cleo added sugar to her coffee. "I know it's rude to say since she just died, but Vivian wasn't a nice person. I mean, she was nice to me. People are almost always nice to someone who can make them look good. Or fry all their hair off." She grinned. "Overall, though, Vivian had a reputation for making nasty little comments. Sometimes under her breath, sometimes really loud in public places. Even louder than I tend to be." Cleo took a tiny sip of her coffee, winced as if it was hot, and set the cup back down. "Right off the bat, I'd think her husband, Phil, is a suspect. They're in the middle of a really bitter divorce."

I wrote the heading "Suspects" on my notepad and began the list with "1. Phil, Vivian's husband."

"He's an accountant," Alice said. "Works for Dwight."

Interesting. I added a comment to my notes. "But if Phil and Vivian were getting a divorce, why would he want to kill her? Even if he hated being married to her, it was going to end." I tapped my pen on the table and thought about my own ex. I hadn't contemplated murdering the man, but if he'd, say, come down in hives or boils or leprosy, I wouldn't have complained. "Unless Vivian had made Phil really angry... Did she cheat on him?"

Cleo pushed her bangs off her forehead, and they magically fell back into place. "I don't think so. At least, if she did, she never mentioned another man when she was getting her hair done. And she kept the same hairstyle for the past several years. Sometimes, when someone comes in wanting a new look, I get the feeling their marriage is in trouble."

I leaned back in my chair and looked over at her. Hairdressers really did know everything about their clients. "Do you think Vivian might have met Phil at the museum so they could discuss how they were dividing their assets, and he decided he'd rather kill her and have them all?"

"No," Alice said. "I heard Vivian talking at the museum about a week ago. She said that the lawyers had worked everything out and that she planned to speak to Phil as little as possible." She took a long drink of coffee and glanced upward, eyes closed, as if savoring a moment of bliss.

I added more numbers to my list, ready to fill in names. "If we look at opportunity, whoever killed Vivian had to be either an employee or a member of the board of directors of the museum. Someone who had a key."

Alice set down her cup. "Some former board member might have a key, but in general, yes, that makes sense."

Cleo leaned in. "It could have been someone Vivian let into the museum. Or someone Imani let in."

"That's true. I need to talk to Imani and find out if anyone had been there before I arrived."

"I bet she's at home." Alice explained that Imani's husband ran a woodworking shop and that when she wasn't at the museum, Imani helped run the retail side. "My neighbor told me John Harper questioned her at the police station for more than two hours but didn't keep her."

"Excellent. I'll stop by. I'd think she'd be glad to know someone thinks she's innocent."

"I'm sure she would." Alice looked up, and conversation

paused as the server set down my tea, Zeke's soda, and our plates. Oatmeal and berries for Alice, stacks of pancakes for Cleo and Zeke, and eggs, bacon, and an English muffin for me.

"What do you know about things at the museum, Alice? Do you think the curator, Rodney, or anyone on the board would have a reason to kill Vivian?"

Alice took a bite of oatmeal and sat for a moment, eyes narrowed.

I added Rodney and—to be fair—Imani to my list. With Phil, that brought us up to three suspects.

"Well," Alice said at last, "I can't picture Rodney Grant killing anyone. We've sung together in the church choir for twenty-odd years." She rubbed her chin. "But some of the members of the board ... goodness, I hate to say this out loud..."

"We can't spare people's feelings if we're going to help Imani," Cleo said.

"You're right." Alice gave a tight nod. "I think I'd be far more likely to suspect someone on the board than I would Rodney or Imani."

Now we were getting somewhere. "Tell me about the other board members." I was pretty sure I'd met all of them except Dwight when I interviewed, but I hadn't learned much about them.

Alice sat back and steepled her hands under her chin. "Well, there's Dwight, of course. He was at the museum yesterday morning."

I wrote him down as Suspect No. 4.

"He always seems on top of things in board meetings," Alice said.

"Um-hmmm." I wrote a comment next to his name. "As the new director, I like that, but he certainly had opportunity to kill Vivian. He could have been at the museum long before I arrived and then made sure we saw him in case the police found his fingerprints at the scene." Not to mention the feeling I had that he was hiding something.

"True." Alice took a sip of her coffee and wiped her mouth with her napkin. "The newest member of the board is Andy Lane. He runs a used car lot north of town. I'm not really sure he knows that much about history. I got the idea that he just thought helping the museum was a good way to serve the community."

"Even Vivian couldn't fault him for wanting to help the town," Cleo said. "She might have been snitty about his ignorance, though."

Alice shook her head. "I'm not sure that would have bothered him. He always struck me as"—she paused—"as well adjusted. Comfortable with his shortcomings and pleased with what he'd made of himself."

I added Andy Lane, car dealer, as No. 5 on my list and put a question mark after his name. Not a very likely suspect, at least on first appearances.

"Terry Kramer, on the other hand, would have been incensed if Vivian implied he was ignorant of anything. He's a local attorney and the vice president of the board." Alice leaned toward me as I wrote down his name, spelling Kramer aloud for me.

I added Terry Kramer, attorney, as Suspect No. 6 and looked back up.

"But I can't imagine Vivian implying Terry was stupid," Alice said. "He's clever but in a way that always made me a bit uncomfortable. Like he'd do anything, right or wrong, to win a case." Alice bit her lip. "But don't repeat that. I feel bad saying it."

Cleo and I assured her our conversation was confidential.

"Anyway, Vivian seemed a little in awe of Terry. I think a time or two she'd tried to make one of her snippy comments at him, and he retaliated in kind." Alice scooped up another bite of oatmeal. "But I can't imagine Terry killing her. It's a weird thing to say, but he wouldn't need to. In the dynamic between the two of them, it felt like he had the power."

"That makes sense." I checked my notebook. "So, you, Dwight, Andy, Terry, and two more board members? I know there are six, but I can't remember all the names."

Alice looked down at my notebook. "There's Mortimer Townsend."

"I know his wife," Cleo said. "She's really nice."

"They both are," Alice agreed. "He's the dean of arts and science at Grove University. He was a history professor before he moved into administration."

That rang a bell. "Oh, yes, I remember him. Vivian was really excited that he had joined the board. Recently, right?"

"About six weeks ago." Alice scooped a berry from her bowl with her spoon. "The Townsends have only been here a few months. Vivian pulled out all the stops to woo him to join. Even had a dinner catered at the museum one evening to impress him. I can't imagine him killing her. As dean, I'm sure he deals with lots of people even more difficult than Vivian. Those faculty members can have quite the egos from what I've seen."

I wrote down Mortimer Townsend, dean, as Suspect No. 7 and sank back in my chair. We weren't making nearly as much progress as I'd hoped. I'd imagined a suspect with obvious means, motive, and opportunity. But maybe figuring that out took more time. "The last board member is a woman, affiliated with the Wild Woods Winery, right?"

Alice nodded. "Co-owner. That's Maria Wilder. She's been on the board for a couple of years now. She has all sorts of good ideas, but Vivian never seemed to like them."

"How strange." Back at the Henry C. Branch House, if we'd had a board member with innovative ideas, we'd have been thrilled. I added Maria Wilder, vintner, to my list as Suspect No. 8 and looked back up at Alice.

"I think Vivian felt threatened by her. Maria was younger, prettier, and I'd say smarter than Vivian. But she never seemed to care when Vivian rejected her ideas. I imagine she has her hands full with the winery. I'm pretty sure the museum board was, for her, like Andy, a way to look good in the community."

"So, no reason for her to want to kill Vivian," Cleo said. "At least nothing that jumps out."

"No." Alice took another sip of coffee, and twin lines

appeared between her eyebrows. "Which in an odd way is disappointing."

I read through my list of suspects. We had Vivian's husband, Phil. Two museum employees, Imani Jones and Rodney Grant. And—if we left out Alice—five members of the board: Dwight the CPA, Andy the car dealer, Terry the attorney, Mortimer the dean, and Maria the vintner. Not knowing any of them well, it was just a list of names that didn't have meaning. I needed to meet people, talk to them, and see if I could discover any clues.

I tapped my pen against the paper. "So, if we rule out Alice, we have eight suspects with opportunity, but only Phil seems to have a motive, other than people disliking Vivian for her general nastiness." This was harder than I'd thought. I consoled myself with a large bite of bacon.

"Maybe you can look through Vivian's email," Cleo said.

I let out a dejected sigh. "Rodney told me the police took her office computer."

"Bummer," Cleo said.

"You can get the emails off the server," Zeke said. "All you need is the administrator password."

Cleo, Alice, and I swung our heads to face him.

How much of our conversation had he heard? "I, uh, I don't know that I have the password. I imagine that was one of the things Vivian planned to tell me when we met."

Zeke slid out his earbuds. "I bet I can hack the password."

"Oh." I twisted the corner of my napkin in my lap. Did I want help from a teenage hacker? Probably so, if it meant I could figure out who the real killer was. "Well, thanks, I guess."

"I want the museum open again. One of my friends really likes it there." Zeke looked back down at his phone.

"A girl," Cleo mouthed to Alice and me.

"That would be great, Zeke. I'd appreciate it." I pulled out my own phone and checked for messages. "Detective Harper still hasn't said we can go in the building, but as soon as I'm allowed, I'll go through the file cabinet in Vivian's office and find any information on the computer system that she saved."

Cleo gave her nephew a look of approval. "Thanks, kid. Who knows? You might find us a great clue." She glanced at the rest of us. "As for me, I'll keep my ears open while I'm at the shop today."

"I'll do the same at altar guild," Alice said.

"And I'll go talk to Imani. If someone else was in the museum yesterday morning, it gives us another suspect." I smiled at the three of them. It was harder than I'd imagined, trying to investigate a murder where I didn't know people, but we were a team, and we had definitely made some progress. "I really appreciate you helping me. Together, maybe we can figure this out."

We paid our bills at the counter, and Cleo and Zeke headed off to her salon.

Alice and I quickly planned an emergency meeting for the museum board that evening so that we could figure out how to respond to Vivian's killing. Alice offered to host the meeting at her home and notify the board. I gladly took her up on it. I'd spend some time before the meeting brain-storming how the museum should respond, but first, I wanted to talk to Imani.

The best way to deal with the public relations nightmare the museum was facing was to find Vivian's killer.

Chapter Five

SHORTLY AFTER ONE, I stopped by the police station and signed my statement, then followed the directions on my phone's GPS to a modest, white, ranch-style house south of town. A separate one-story shop sat beside the house. Although neither building was large, they looked as well kept as something on HGTV. When I took off my sunglasses, I could see that the grass had actually been cut in two directions, creating a checkerboard effect.

Once inside, I found more checkerboard patterns, beautifully crafted from light and dark woods into chopping boards. The checkerboards, though impressive, were only the beginning of the gorgeous offerings of the store.

I waved to Imani, who was helping a customer, and wandered over to another display of chopping boards, these featuring floral shapes created from darker wood and imbedded in the boards. I peeked at the price of a mid-sized board and quickly dropped the tag. Ninety dollars for a chopping board was far beyond my budget.

I admired wood carvings of water birds as Imani gift-wrapped a package. As soon as the customer left, I approached the counter. "Imani, how are you doing?"

"I'm ... okay." She straightened a pile of brochures on the counter.

I glanced around to make sure no one else was in the store. "I wanted to stop by and tell you that I know you didn't kill Vivian. You were as shocked as I was when we found her."

Imani's face crumpled. "Thank you." She dug into the pocket of her short canvas skirt, pulled out a tissue, and wiped her nose. "It means a lot to hear you say that."

"I tried to tell Detective Harper, but—"

"But he thinks I killed her." Imani's words tumbled out. "I mean, I know some things make me look bad, like I did touch the body. He says I did that on purpose, to make sure I had an excuse for having my DNA at the scene."

"You touched the body because you were trying to see if she was still alive." I blew out an irritated breath. "We both checked for a pulse. And wouldn't your DNA have been there anyway? I assume you and Vivian sometimes met in her office."

"We did, but he's got other things he holds against me. Somebody told him that Vivian threatened to fire me a week ago because of how I messed up the last email campaign to the member list."

See? I knew I was right to trust her. If she were dishonest, she wouldn't be volunteering that information. "What happened?"

"The system we're using is ancient, but Vivian hated to spend money on technology. Dale—that's my husband—and I have an email list for the shop. We send out an email when he has a new line or we're doing something special for the holidays. It's really easy to use, but the system at work..."

"That seems like something we should evaluate. It might be worth the money to upgrade."

"Well, actually, after the giant mess I made, Alice made a donation specifically to fund a new system until the beginning of the next calendar year. She thinks it will more than pay for itself in increased donations and the time we will save."

"Wow. I've only gotten to know her a little, but Alice seems like such an asset to the museum."

"She really is. She'd make a great director if she wanted the job." Imani covered her mouth with her hand. "I mean, um, she volunteers all over town," Imani said quickly. "The museum on Mondays, the hospital on Fridays, and sometime in between, her church and the food pantry and the library. She wouldn't be able to work full-time. And I'm sure you'll be a great director." She paused for breath. "That's why I made a special effort to get to the museum early yesterday. Because I'm excited to have the chance to work with you. And hoping you don't fire me." She clasped her hands under her chin.

"I have no intention of firing you." Not after I'd learned

the hard way how awful it felt to lose a job. Besides, for all I knew, the problem had been Vivian. Imani deserved a second chance. "We'll talk about the problems you had, and if the new email system doesn't fix them, we'll try to come up with another way to make things work better." I patted her shoulder. "After all, with Vivian gone, I'm going to need all the help you can give me to figure out my new job."

"Thank you." Imani looked down, then wiped a tear from her cheek. "Detective Harper even acted like my coming in early yesterday made me seem guilty. Because Rodney must have told him I've been late a lot lately. Pretty much every day. But..."

She seemed unsure whether to go on.

I forced myself to stay silent. I wanted to know everything that had been going on at the museum, but if I pushed too hard, she might clam up and not tell me anything.

Imani lowered her voice. "I shouldn't be telling you this. We wanted to wait another week before we told anyone, but... I'm pregnant. I've been late to work a lot because I've been having horrible morning sickness."

"Oh." My breath came out in a whoosh. "I'm sorry you've been feeling poorly, but congratulations." I stepped to the side of the counter and gave her a quick hug.

"The doctor says that most likely she'll stop getting sick every morning in another week or two. I sure hope so." A tall man with vivid blue eyes, dark blond hair, and a thick beard walked in from a room behind the desk. "Dale Jones," he said, sticking out a hand.

We shook as I introduced myself, then I congratulated him on his upcoming baby.

"Thanks. And I was working in the back and heard you talking. Thanks for coming by to tell Imani you believe she's innocent. She told the detective about her morning sickness, but—"

"But I don't think he understood how awful it is," Imani finished.

"Anyway, there's no way Imani would have killed Vivian, although I'm sure lots of people were secretly glad to see her gone." Dale twisted his mouth into a grimace. With his height, strong build, plaid shirt, thick beard, and that expression, he looked like an angry lumberjack. "That woman was mean."

He didn't sound threatening, but I instinctively took a half step back. "Is, uh, is there anyone specific who comes to mind? I'm not sure how we can reopen if people think a murderer is still hanging around the museum." I stood up taller and told myself to stop babbling. "If there's anything I can do to help the police, I feel it's my duty as the director."

Dale glanced out the front window of the shop. A minivan had pulled into the parking lot. "Nah. A lot of people might hate her, but I can't think of anyone who would actually murder Vivian."

"Me either," Imani said. "People in Dogwood Springs are nice. They don't go around killing each other."

I looked at her and raised one eyebrow.

She fiddled with the opening to the pocket of her skirt. "Well, not most of the time."

"What about opportunity?" I'd almost forgotten to ask. "Was anyone else at the museum yesterday morning?"

The bell on the front door jangled, and Dale tipped his head toward the back room. "Why don't you show Libby the workshop, Imani? I'll man the desk for a bit."

"Oh, sorry." I backed away from the counter. Everyone in town had probably heard about Imani being questioned, but if the customer was a tourist, the last thing they needed to hear was that one of the owners of the shop was suspected of murder.

Imani pointed to the door behind the counter. "Let's go back here. I'll show you what Dale's making for the baby."

We walked through the door into a large workshop. The smell of fresh-cut wood and varnish was stronger than in the sales area, and the room was filled with lumber, works in progress, and tools I'd never be able to name. Imani proudly showed me Dale's latest project, a beautiful crib he was creating out of maple.

"It's gorgeous." I ran a finger over the top rail of the crib, already sanded silky smooth, and turned to Imani. "But was anyone in the building yesterday morning before I got there?"

"Actually, yes. But I can't in a million years imagine that he killed Vivian."

I was getting a little tired of people telling me that potential suspects couldn't have killed Vivian. Everyone couldn't be innocent. The woman was dead. "Who was it?"

"When Alice paid for the new email system, she arranged for a friend of hers, a computer science professor at the university, to come in and move the list over. With the weird old system we had, I was really unsure about the transfer. I talked to this guy, and he said he could do it in about ten minutes. And he did. Every name moved, with all the data in the right fields and everything."

Alice hadn't mentioned this, but maybe she hadn't known when he had come. "Were you with him the whole time while he worked?"

"No. I, um, I had to run to the bathroom. I'd eaten the lightest breakfast I could, but..." Imani touched her abdomen and made an awkward gesture with her hands.

"So, he could have killed Vivian without you even knowing it."

She wrinkled her nose. "I guess."

"What about a motive? Did he even know Vivian, do you think?"

"Well, yeah, he did. I heard them arguing one day last week in her office."

"Really? Did you tell the police?"

"I did tell the detective that the professor had been in, but I didn't think about the argument until last night."

"What was it about?"

"He found a painting of people in Dogwood Springs in an old house he bought. He thought it was really valuable and wanted to donate it to the museum and get a tax write-off. Vivian said she wouldn't be a party to fraud. She told him the painting was worthless, but he didn't believe her."

"How valuable did he think it was?"

"He thought it might be worth a quarter of a million dollars."

I raised a hand to my chest. "A quarter of a million dollars? That's motive, Imani. A lot of motive." Especially if he thought that, because of the location of the painting, this museum was the only one that would want it.

"Maybe, but I think he's really well off, and I got the impression he didn't want to be arguing with her. Vivian was"—Imani ran a hand over her mouth—"prickly. You could start the most innocent conversation, and suddenly, she'd insult you, and you felt like yelling."

"Still, a quarter of a million dollars." This felt like a real lead, at last.

Imani scrunched up her face. "But why kill Vivian yesterday? Why not last week?"

"Hmmm. You might have a point." Even so, I should talk with this guy and subtly ask where he was at the time of the crime. "What's his name?"

"Sam. Sam Collins."

I pulled out my notebook, wrote it down, and added that he taught computer science at the local college. Then I told Imani about the board meeting planned for that evening. "I'm hoping we can work from home, at least for a while."

"Thank you. I'd feel a lot safer that way."

"Me too. You take it easy, try to get over the morning sickness, and I'll let you know what we decide."

Another customer came in, and Imani thanked me for coming by and hurried off to discuss chopping boards.

Time for me to visit Grove University.

Chapter Six

A BUBBLE of pride welled up in my chest as I parked in a visitor's lot at Grove University. When my great-great grand-mother Elsie Dorsett had been mayor of the town back in the 1920s, she'd worked hard to attract businesses that fit her ideal of a lovely community, including encouraging a local railroad baron to fund Grove University, which had started as a small teachers' college. The charming campus, with its red-brick buildings surrounding a classic college green, was part of Elsie's legacy.

Of course, I wasn't going to mention that to Sam Collins. And I had no guarantee he'd even be in his office, but, as with Imani, I thought an unannounced visit would be best.

Luck was on my side. I found a campus map on my phone and followed it to the computer science building. Right inside the door, I spotted a list of faculty members and their office numbers. I took the stairs to the second floor. Collins's door was open, and bits of conversation floated out.

I waited quietly in the hall while he explained a homework problem to a student. After they talked it through, the student seemed to understand the concept. He thanked Collins, tossed out a plea for him to make the upcoming exam easy, and left, not even noticing me.

I hitched my bag higher on my shoulder and knocked. "Professor Collins?"

"Come in."

Inside, I found the typical faculty office—walls lined with books and a desk piled with paper—except that Collins's desk held three computer monitors and was surrounded by additional stacks of paper.

He was maybe forty, dark haired with rectangular glasses, and good looking enough that I expected a few female students took his courses simply for the scenery. He stood, rising to over six feet, and gestured to the chair across from him. "Please, call me Sam. How can I help you?"

"I'm Libby Ballard, the new director of the Dogwood Springs History Museum. I understand you've been helping us get our email system upgraded. I was on campus and wanted to thank you."

He shrugged. "It was nothing. Alice VanMeter said you needed some help, and I was happy to set things up. I think you'll find the new system is a real improvement. I have no idea why Vivian resisted the change."

"I guess we'll never know." I spoke slowly, watching carefully for his reaction.

"True." He pressed his fingertips against his lips. "I should have offered my condolences. Quite shocking, a murder here in Dogwood Springs."

I nodded. His chocolate-brown eyes held no guilt, simply the appropriate level of sympathy. Overall, he looked kind and friendly. And handsome. Did I mention he was handsome?

But that was not what I should be thinking, given that he was one of the suspects in my investigation. And as I knew all too well from my marriage, a handsome man could be synonymous with betrayal, financial hardship, and heartache.

Sam cleared his throat.

Some smooth investigator I was. I'd let the conversation awkwardly drop. "Uh, I wasn't expecting a major crime when I took the position, I assure you. But I, uh, I understand you have a painting you're interested in donating."

"I do." His face brightened. "Vivian said it was a fake, but I think it might be a work by Clayton Smithton."

"Really?" A Clayton Smithton painting could easily be worth a quarter of a million. "What's the subject?"

"It looks like a family—mom, dad, and a daughter. There's nothing on the back to say who the people are, and I imagine, if they had descendants, they'd have kept it. I thought the museum would be eager to have it as part of its collection, but Vivian wasn't at all interested."

"Someone mentioned that the two of you had a rather heated discussion."

Sam's eyes narrowed.

I shifted in my chair, pretty sure I'd blown my story of stopping by only to thank him for computer help.

He tipped his head to one side. "She struck me as an odd choice for a role that's largely development. She was downright rude during that conversation." He pressed a hand against his mouth, then released it. "But I shouldn't speak ill of the dead."

If I wanted to keep up the pretense of why I'd come to his office, I'd better change the subject. "Where did you find the painting?"

"Way back in a closet under the eaves in my new house. Well, new to me. It's a big old Victorian."

"Which house?" With the resources at the museum, I could research who'd built it, maybe search Smithton's works for that family name.

"It's out east of town, a place called Ashlington."

My mouth fell open. "Ashlington? You bought Ashlington?"

"Yes, do you know it?"

"Very well. It was my Aunt Gloria who sold it to you." But when my mom said the place had been bought by a retired computer mogul, I'd pictured someone in his sixties.

"Wow. Small world." Sam leaned back in his chair. "It's an amazing property. I wanted it mostly for the views. I wasn't totally sure I'd like living in a house that old."

I squelched a protest and tried to keep my face arranged in a pleasant expression. But the very idea that someone who didn't like history was living at Ashlington made a knot form in my chest.

"The more I've been there, though, the more I love it. It feels"—he hesitated—"I know this is going to sound weird, but the sense of history is almost palpable, as if the walls hold memories of lots of happy times."

The tightness in my chest eased. He did appreciate it after all. "I'm glad you like the place. And, yes, there were many happy times there."

"Good to know I wasn't imagining it." He sat up taller. "I've been doing some renovations."

"I—" I stopped myself before I mentioned that I'd driven by and seen the scaffolding. "The bathrooms? I remember bubble-gum pink tile."

He gave an exaggerated shudder. "Gone. No more pink at all. I had the bathrooms redone in a style that, according to my interior designer, is in keeping with the original character of the house. And I made significant changes in the kitchen." He paused. "Would you like to come out and see the place? I could show you the painting as well."

Did I want to see the house? You bet. But I wasn't sure I wanted to be alone there with someone on my suspect list.

"I should also tell you that I emailed your aunt, sent her a photo of the painting, and told her what I thought it might be worth. But she said that, according to the paperwork, everything conveyed, and she didn't have a place for it down in Texas. She seemed adamant."

I gave a wry smile. "Yeah, that sounds like Aunt Gloria." Fast decisions, adamantly upheld, never-in-a-million-years willing to change her mind.

Although my parents weren't lacking for money, my

mother would be furious if she learned she had missed out on her share of a quarter of a million dollars. I knew better, though, than to get in the middle of a dispute between her and her sisters.

But Sam had tried to make things right. Would a murderer have done that? I didn't think so. I wanted to see the renovations, but I didn't want to be stupid. "Let me check my calendar, and I'll get back with you." I stood and hefted my bag onto my shoulder.

"Sure. I can always bring the painting by the museum if you'd prefer." He made sure I had his contact info and walked with me to the door of his office. "But the invitation stands. I'd love for you to see what I've done with Ashlington."

I headed back to my car, remembering the bathrooms and kitchen at Ashlington, as well as homes in Philadelphia that had been lovingly restored with the help of a skilled designer. Ashlington deserved care like that, and part of me really wanted to see every change that Sam had made. Another part of me, the part that had a better-than-average IQ, silently cheered for self-preservation. The man was on my list of suspects. Being alone with him in his home was not a good idea.

But maybe if I could rule Sam out as the killer, I could take him up on his offer.

I drove home, then walked over to Cleo's salon. As good looking as Sam was, Cleo was bound to know the scoop on him.

Cleo's shop was a spa-like space that would have been right at home in a large city. Instead of stations, it had individual rooms for each stylist. Decorated in shades of muted teal and gray with silver accents, the salon was soothing to every sense—soft instrumental music, restful abstract art, and the faint hint of lavender in the air.

The receptionist told me Cleo was waiting for a client who was running late. A moment later, Cleo led me into her workspace, waved a hand at the salon chair, and sat down on a small bench. "How did things go with Imani?"

I'd almost forgotten about my visit to the woodworking shop. I quickly filled Cleo in on my conversation with Imani and Dale and my visit to see Sam.

"Oh." She leaned back against the wall. "I knew your mom was a Dorsett. I guess everyone in town did. But I hadn't put together that Sam Collins is living in your family home. Quite a hottie, isn't he?"

I gave a reluctant nod.

"Well, I don't care what Imani heard. I can't imagine Sam murdering Vivian over a tax write-off."

"If the painting is an actual Clayton Smithton, it would be one sizable deduction. Probably at least a quarter of a million dollars."

Cleo let out a sound that was half laugh, half snort. "Libby, that man is loaded. A quarter of a million probably means nothing to him. Seriously, he's worth at least half a billion. Billion, with a 'B.'" She traced a capital letter B in the air.

My eyes widened. "What's he doing in Dogwood Springs?"

"Apparently, he ran a huge tech business and burned out completely. Just decided one day that he'd had enough. He sold the business and looked for a job as a professor not too far from St. Louis, where his parents live. I think he only works so he won't be bored."

"So, he's not the murderer, and I'm probably safe going out to see the house?"

"Safe?" She looked at me as if I were refusing gourmet chocolate. "You'd be the envy of every unmarried woman in town. He hasn't dated a soul since he moved here two years ago."

Hmmm. There was a story there, I'd bet. But Sam Collins's status as the most eligible bachelor in town was not my concern. I'd been divorced for six months, separated for eighteen months before that. Some women might have been ready for a new relationship. For me, the thought of dating held about as much appeal as eating one of Bella's dog biscuits.

On the other hand, I would truly love to see what Sam had done to Ashlington. As soon as I had time, I'd call and accept his invitation because Cleo's reasoning made sense. He had no motive to kill Vivian.

In the meantime, I should get ready for the board meeting. Not only did we need a plan to offset the negative publicity from Vivian's death at the museum, but this meeting was also important for my investigation. Maria, Terry, Andy, Mortimer, and Dwight should all be there.

It was the perfect opportunity to discuss Vivian's murder and watch their reactions.

Chapter Seven

A LITTLE BEFORE SEVEN, I turned onto the street near Alice's house and parked behind a white van with the Wild Woods Winery logo on the back. For a moment, I sat in my car, staring at my fingernails. Even without the murder, I would have been nervous heading into my first board meeting. Now, I not only needed to make a good impression and figure out how to navigate what had to be the worst possible PR situation for the museum, but I also had to try to figure out if one of the board members might be a killer. Easy, right?

But being late wouldn't help. I blew out a long breath, climbed out of my car, and scooped up my bag. I'd changed into my second-favorite green blouse and black dress pants and added my pearls for confidence. I brushed some dog hair off my pants, walked toward Alice's lovely two-story brick house, and rang the bell.

Dwight opened the door and waved me inside. "Alice is setting out refreshments. We're in the kitchen."

Inside, the house was equally impressive, with tasteful neutral décor, a collection of modern sculptures, and the healthiest houseplants I'd ever seen. I remembered Vivian telling me Alice's husband ran a business that sold custommade gift baskets online. From the looks of their home, those baskets were a hit.

I followed Dwight down a short hallway and entered a kitchen with a large island with four barstools along one side. Two men and a woman sat at the island.

Alice backed away from the fridge and turned toward me, holding a pitcher of iced tea. "Libby, how nice to see you." She set the pitcher on the island and gestured to the others, one by one. "You remember Mortimer, Andy, and Maria?"

I nodded.

Andy, the younger man, was close to my age. He had curly blond hair and an easy smile and looked as if he might have played football in college. Mortimer was heavyset and probably in his sixties. While Andy had on khakis and a red polo with his car dealership's logo, Mortimer wore a slightly rumpled suit and tie. I greeted them and wondered if I should have worn a jacket and heels instead of flats.

The doorbell rang, and Alice went to answer it.

Maria, a twenty-something brunette with a messy bun, gestured to the bar stool beside her and welcomed me to town. Her words had the faintest hint of an accent that made me think she was originally from Central or South America.

I was grateful to see that she wore a casual skirt and a T-shirt.

"Now that we're all here," Alice said as she and a man I recognized as the last member of the board, who had to be Terry, came into the kitchen.

Terry was dark haired, maybe fifty, and slight of build. He too wore a suit, one that probably cost at least three times as much as Mortimer's.

"Hope I didn't keep you all waiting." Terry poured himself a glass of tea. "I had to drop off my daughter at the high school. She's working on a service project with the National Honor Society." His eyes shone, and his words rang with pride. Clearly, this was a man who loved his daughter.

"You didn't keep us waiting at all." Alice took a dish of fresh lemon slices from the fridge. "I haven't even set everything out yet."

Maria touched my arm. "How are you doing, really? I heard that you and Imani found Vivian's body."

A perfect opening for me to get them talking about the murder. I nodded. "Thanks for asking. I'm okay, but it must be so horrible for Vivian's family and friends." Not that it seemed she had many friends. "I wish I knew why someone would want to kill her."

I glanced around to see if anyone looked guilty, but no such luck.

Terry gave a half shrug, as if he hadn't a clue.

Dwight shook his head and quickly turned to get himself a cup of coffee. Guilty? Or simply uncomfortable with the topic?

Maria looked sympathetic, as if she might be thinking how awkward it was for me to start a new job in the middle of a homicide.

Andy leaned forward, propped an elbow on the island, and turned to me. "I've been wondering myself about the murder. Vivian could be difficult to get along with, but it's hard to imagine someone hating her enough to kill her." His brow furrowed and then released. "Maybe she had money and some relative killed her to inherit."

Dwight turned back to face us. "I didn't do their taxes, and of course I wouldn't say anything if I had, but I never got the impression that either Vivian or Phil was particularly well off."

"Maybe it was something else," Maria said. "Like an extramarital affair gone wrong."

Terry, who had been adding lemon to his tea, looked up. "Honestly, people commit murder for all sorts of reasons. Jealousy. Revenge. Insurance."

All good motives. But no one, with the possible exception of Dwight, seemed uncomfortable with the conversation.

Alice took a gorgeous chocolate cake from a bakery box and set it on a cake stand. "Please, help yourselves. Jackie made this, so you know it's fabulous."

"That's my wife," Dwight said to me in a low voice as we stood.

I glanced at the label on the box. "I've seen her shop downtown. Does she make shortbread, by any chance?"

"She does. I think it's on Wednesdays." Dwight gestured for me to go ahead of him in line for cake.

"I'll have to remember that. Shortbread's my favorite." I poured myself a glass of iced tea and, like the others, took a slice of cake.

In the dining room, Alice pointed me to the head of the table, so I sat, opened my portfolio, and put the day's date at the top of my legal pad. Then I took a bite of cake. It was dark chocolate with a chocolate ganache icing, and I paused for a moment of reverence. When I looked up, everyone was watching me.

"Fabulous, isn't it?" Maria grinned. "No one can figure out why Dwight doesn't weigh four hundred pounds."

Dwight patted his trim waist. "It's the accounting. Lots of calories burned dealing with assets and liabilities."

Everyone laughed.

Now that I'd been around Dwight more, he seemed like a nice guy. Maybe I'd been wrong to suspect him. Maybe that weird feeling I had around him before was simply nerves.

Alice called the meeting to order and asked Andy, who was the secretary for the group, to note that, as this was an emergency meeting, we were skipping routine reports and old business. We paused for a moment of silence remembering Vivian. Then Alice formally introduced me, apologized for the way my position at the museum had begun, and asked me to share my ideas for how to proceed.

We worked our way through the three issues I thought were essential. The group readily agreed that the museum should stay closed until the killer was arrested and that after the police allowed us to go in to get what we needed, Imani, Rodney, and I should work from home. Until then, all staff, me included, would be given paid leave.

Throughout the meeting, I tried to focus not only on the topics we were discussing, but also on what each board member was like. Dwight and Terry were almost stereotypical in their responses. Dwight, a CPA, seemed to focus on the financial aspects of every issue. Terry, a lawyer, didn't really add much but seemed to enjoy hearing himself talk.

Maria suggested that I only communicate with potential donors by mail for the time being.

Dwight's face tensed. "But the cost of that unnecessary postage—"

She cut him off. "We don't have that many potential donors, and that way," she said to me, "you won't get sucked into difficult conversations. With email or a phone call, someone might ask how the murder investigation is going or ask who found the body. We don't want donors thinking about that. We want them excited about the idea of a new director with experience at a place as prestigious as the Henry C. Branch House."

"A great idea." I made a note on my pad. I certainly didn't want to relive seeing Vivian's body. A letter would also let me carefully word things to gloss over why I'd left my previous position, focusing on my family connection to Dogwood Springs.

Mortimer suggested that as soon as the police allowed anyone back in the building, I get new locks put in. He also suggested that, until an arrest was made and we officially reopened, only Alice, as the board president, and me should have keys. Some of the board members initially seemed surprised, as if they'd never thought they might be considered suspects. But after a moment or two, everyone agreed.

Andy's idea, that Imani use the time at home to do any available training on the new email service, was also a good one. I liked the fact that he, as well as the rest of the board, appeared to be ignoring the initial rumors of Imani's guilt as well as Vivian's plan to fire her. All in all, the board seemed supportive, understanding of the fact that the situation was uniquely challenging for me, and focused on helping the museum succeed.

I was no closer to figuring out who might have killed Vivian, but I left the meeting energized.

The next morning, just after eight, I called Rodney and Imani and told them that the board had voted to give them paid time off until we were allowed back in the museum. Then, because the weatherman was predicting a scorcher, I decided to take Bella for an extra-long walk. Better to get all our exercise in early. We started on our regular route, down Elm, but instead of turning at Thirteenth Street, I gave the leash a tug, encouraging her to continue on.

Bella happily walked with me to Eighteenth Street, where I told her we needed to cross and head home.

On the way back, in the 1100 block, I spotted the name "P. Martin" on a mailbox.

In a town this small, P. Martin was most likely Phil Martin, Vivian's husband. Bella and I had walked past the house several times, but I'd never noticed it. I'd had no idea that one of the people I suspected might have killed Vivian lived so close.

The house was an attractive, brown, story-and-a-half Craftsman probably built before World War I. I'd gotten a vague idea of local housing prices when I looked for apartments. That place had to be worth at least $200,000, even in Dogwood Springs, and if Vivian and Phil's divorce hadn't been final at the time of her death, it probably belonged entirely to him now. And something Terry had said last night, about life insurance, popped into my mind.

I rolled the idea of insurance in my head as Bella and I finished our walk. Back home, I ran into Cleo as she loaded items she planned to donate to charity into the back of her old red Jeep. I filled her in on the meeting the night before.

"I was stymied on the investigation when I got home, but while Bella and I were out, I thought of something. We should be looking at who benefits from Vivian's death financially."

Cleo's eyes widened. "Good idea. Well, we know the property in the divorce was pretty much settled. But if her husband, Phil, wasn't happy with how things had worked out, I guess that could be motive."

"Or what about life insurance? I wonder if she had a policy and who the beneficiary was."

Cleo shut the back of her Jeep and looked up with a gleam in her eyes. "You're in luck there. One of my clients is the secretary at the biggest agency in town and has a tendency to be"—Cleo cleared her throat—"a little chatty, shall we say. Let me give her a call." She walked over to the stairs to her apartment and sat down.

While Cleo made her phone call, I left her watching Bella and hauled my trash to the curb.

I returned just as Cleo hung up, her eyes wide. "Phil is still the beneficiary. And get this. The policy was for a million dollars."

I sank back on my heels. "A million dollars? Why so much?"

"My client doesn't know. But she did say that both Phil and Vivian had million-dollar policies."

That certainly gave Phil motive. "But what about the fact that Vivian never wanted to see Phil again? Why would she let him into the museum when—"

Cleo held up a hand to stop me. "Wait. I think I know the answer to that. Their dog. I hadn't put it together until now, but I heard from a client yesterday afternoon that Phil got the dog in the divorce. No matter how rude she could be to people, Vivian loved that dog. It's got cancer, and they've been taking it to Columbia, to the vet school at Mizzou, for treatment. Vivian agreed that Phil could keep the dog because she wanted it to continue with that vet, who's apparently one of the top in his field."

"How sad that the dog is so sick."

When I said the word *dog*, Bella trotted over to me. Such a smart girl. I rubbed her ears. She'd only been with me a few days, but I was amazed at how bright she was. And by how important she already was to me.

"Well, the vet at Mizzou is really good, so hopefully the dog will get better," Cleo said. "And my client told me that part of the divorce agreement is that if the dog improves, Vivian gets to have it half of every year in Florida with her. Anyway, if Phil had brought the dog by, I know Vivian would have let him in."

That made sense. "He wouldn't even have to bring the dog. Just say that he did."

"Exactly." Cleo nodded. "And if he got away with the murder, he'd get everything that had been divided in the divorce agreement, the life insurance, and the dog, year round."

"Then I think I need to pay a visit to Phil. C'mon, Bella, let's go inside."

"Wait." Cleo stood up. "We need to go see him together. You don't want to be like one of those stupid heroines on TV."

I hesitated. I knew the TV characters she meant. Like the woman who'd hear a noise in the attic in the middle of the night when the power was out and go up to investigate, carrying a candle that could go out at any minute.

When a serial killer was on the loose.

That never ended well.

I looked over at Cleo. "When are you free today?"

Her eyes lit. "Let me check." She pulled her phone from her back pocket and tapped the screen. Her lips turned down, and she jabbed the screen again and again, her frown deepening. "Not until after seven. I don't even know when I'm going to eat lunch." She shoved the phone back in her pocket. "Maybe you should tell Detective Harper about the insurance."

"I don't know. I feel as if I need more. I don't want him to brush aside my suspicions, not giving them any more credence than he gave my assertions that Imani couldn't have committed the murder." I looked at Bella, rolling in the grass. "And I would be going to Phil's office in broad daylight."

"We-ell-l," Cleo said slowly. "That is true."

"Besides, I learned my lesson yesterday with Sam. I wasn't sneaky enough, and I think he figured out I wasn't really there to thank him for helping Imani with the email list. So, I won't ask Phil anything directly. I'll offer my condolences and get a feel for how he responds."

"You'll be careful?"

"I promise. And if I learn anything I think the detective will act on or I feel in any danger, I won't even leave the building. I'll go out in the lobby, where I'm around other people, and call him."

Cleo worried her lower lip.

She was a good friend to be so concerned about me. Having gotten to know her somewhat, I had a feeling that if the situation were reversed, she'd have charged in without a second thought. "I'll be fine." I gave her my most convincing smile, called to Bella, and went in my kitchen door.

Chapter Eight

MY CONFIDENCE FALTERED AS SOON as I entered the lobby of Bower, Baker, and Martin, Certified Public Accountants.

Did I really want to talk to Phil? Alone? Wouldn't it be smarter to turn around, walk out, and go straight to Detective Harper?

No, I needed something more tangible, the proverbial "hard evidence" to take to the detective. And what I'd told Cleo made sense. Phil wouldn't commit murder in his office during business hours. Not with all these people around.

Dwight, Phil, and their partner had quite a nice business. Four clients waited in a well-appointed tan and navy seating area, a coffee bar at the side of the lobby offered a premium brand and fresh donuts, and a pair of women sat behind a glass window, diligently staring at computer screens and tapping at their keyboards.

I squared my shoulders, hitched up my purse, and

approached the window. Moments later, Phil came out, introduced himself, led me to his office, and offered me a chair.

He was short, no more than five foot seven, and the only word to describe him was round. Round head with a bald spot on top and a gray fringe of hair on the sides, round muddy-brown eyes, and a round tummy like Santa. His office, which appeared to have been decorated at the same time as the lobby, displayed only two things that gave insight into his personality—a plaque from the Dogwood Springs Country Club, proclaiming him the winner of a recent golf tournament, and what looked like a professional photo of a black dachshund.

I introduced myself and explained that I was Vivian's successor as director of the museum. "I wanted to stop by and offer my condolences," I said, trying to sound sincere. "I'm so sorry for your loss."

Most people might not offer condolences to someone involved in an ugly divorce, but I was new in town. How was he to know that I knew his marriage was over?

"Thank you." He exhaled and deflated into his chair. "That's very kind of you. We were actually getting divorced, but even with all her faults, Viv didn't deserve to be killed like that."

Hmmm. He didn't act guilty. Perhaps I should pry a tiny bit more. I shifted in my chair, trying to figure out what to say next. "It was so shocking. From what the police say, I was out walking my dog when it happened, blithely enjoying the morning and thinking what a lovely town this is."

He nodded slowly. "I know how you feel. I was out of the office, doing an audit, thinking it was a typical Monday."

Was it my imagination, or was he deliberately making sure I knew he had an alibi? And how good of an alibi was it? He could have killed Vivian, then driven to the location of the audit. But he hadn't said one single thing I could use as solid proof.

The air conditioning kicked on violently, as if it needed some sort of repair, and I jerked.

It shifted to a loud hum, letting out a *clank* every few seconds.

Phil shrugged, and I assumed the noise was a chronic issue. For a business that spent so much on decorating, I'd have thought they'd keep their HVAC in better repair. On the other hand, maybe they were on a long waiting list for a repairman. The high temperatures the past few days had probably wreaked havoc on lots of air-conditioners.

I had one more avenue of questions I could try. I angled my head toward the photo on the credenza. "What a nice-looking dog."

He gazed at the photo, and his face brightened. "That's Oscar. For 'Oscar Mayer Weiner.' He's been having some health issues, but Doc Parsons over at Dogwood Springs Veterinary recommended a specialist who's really helping him."

"Parsons? I'll have to remember the name. I recently adopted a dog."

"If you're looking for a vet, Susie Parsons is great."

"Thanks for the recommendation." I stood. "Please let me know when Vivian's funeral is arranged. I'm sure everyone connected to the museum will want to attend."

His jaw tightened.

Was that a sign of guilt? Did he wonder if Vivian's coworkers would miss her? Or did he simply wonder why this strange woman was in his office?

"Information about the arrangements should be in the paper tomorrow," he said.

I thanked him again and left. Once outside the building, I hurried down the sidewalk, rounded a corner, and stopped under the shade of a large maple. My visit had either been borderline rude or potentially dangerous. Either way, it was just plain awkward. Perhaps I should have listened to Cleo.

I wanted to solve this murder, wanted to make the museum a safe place for the visitors and staff, but I didn't know what to do next. I couldn't expect the killer to come out and confess.

Dejected, I went home, made a half-hearted attempt at writing a letter to potential donors, once again brushed Bella's coat until it shone, and fixed some frozen enchiladas.

After dinner, on a whim, I pulled up the contact information for Sam Collins on my phone. It was a little after seven, and the long summer evening stretched before me, the perfect time to visit Ashlington and see the possible Clayton Smithton painting, if Sam was available.

He was.

～

Twenty minutes later, I pulled up the long gravel driveway at Ashlington.

The scaffolding was gone, and bright white trim gleamed against the pale peach house. It truly was a beautiful place. I gazed at the wide porch, the balcony above, and the turret and thought of the stories of Great-Great-Grandma Elsie that would be so much richer if told in the home where she had grown up. A bubble of excitement rose in my chest.

Maybe, after the killer was caught and things were running smoothly at the museum, I could start a tour of historic homes in Dogwood Springs to benefit the museum. Staff and volunteers could share area history, homeowners could show off their houses, and the museum could build up some cash.

I filed away the idea, then got out of my car, climbed the wide wooden stairs to the porch, and approached the front door. I raised my hand to knock, and an odd bundle of nerves twisted in my gut. Which was silly. Sam Collins was no longer a suspect and posed no danger to me. I rapped loudly on the door.

A minute later, he pulled it open, and a broad smile spread across his face. "Welcome!"

I swallowed. The nerves in my stomach were back, and they had nothing at all to do with a murder investigation.

Sam looked even more handsome in jeans and a St. Louis Cardinal's T-shirt than he had in khakis and a polo. Suddenly, I was glad I'd changed out of shorts and into a casual dress.

He gestured to the front entryway. "Look familiar?"

A wave of longing washed through my heart as I took in the familiar hardwood floor, the sparkling chandelier, and the wide, curving staircase that led upstairs. "It does. I'm really glad you haven't changed this. There were so many family photos taken on that staircase."

"I think my designer would quit if I even mentioned changes to the staircase. She's great with giving me lots of options, but she also makes it clear that there are some aspects of the architecture that are sacred." He took a step toward the living room. "Come see the mantel."

The mantel, which had been white as long as I remembered, was now finished with a dark stain and glowed in the soft evening light that came through the tall windows.

"We had to remove about six coats of paint. It was so thick that the carvings were indistinct. When the paint was gone, my designer said it was criminal to cover up the original walnut. She said it had been stained, not painted, when the house was first built, so even though I liked the white, that's what we went with."

I glanced over at him with new respect.

"Don't act so surprised." He laughed, then grew more serious. "A place like this isn't just a house, it's a responsibility. I want it to reflect me"—he pointed to an enormous

TV and a long, tan, leather couch—"by being easy to live in, but I don't want to obliterate its history."

A blanket of warmth encircled my heart. Sam was not only handsome, he had an appreciation for history.

But then, so did my ex.

And I needed to focus on Ashlington. "This is lovely. I can't wait to see the rest."

Sam took me through the whole house. The renovated bathrooms, which perfectly blended modern convenience and historic design elements. The patio off the library, where he'd clearly dropped a large handful of cash on landscaping. And the bedrooms, still structurally much the same but with different wall colors and furnishings. If I noticed a shirt sleeve sticking out from under the closet door in the master bedroom, as if Sam had made a quick attempt to clean, I didn't let on. Frankly, it was rather flattering to think he might have tidied up for my visit.

We went back downstairs to the kitchen, which had been completely transformed.

"I know this is a big change." He gave me a sideways glance. "Over the past year, I've been learning to cook. Not just scrambled eggs and frozen pizza, but really cook. So, I wanted a great kitchen."

The old butler's pantry had been ripped out, expanding the space by at least a third, and the enlarged space featured green marble countertops, white cabinets with decorative detailing, and a long row of copper pots and kettles. "It's fabulous."

"I'm glad you like it." He grinned.

"I love it. I love everything you've done. In fact, don't tell Aunt Gloria, but I think you're taking better care of the house than she did."

"Thank you. That means a lot." He angled his head to one side. "Ready to see the painting?"

"Definitely." A little flutter of excitement built in my chest. Wouldn't it be something if it was real? If the museum could have a Clayton Smithton on display? That would definitely bring in the tourists.

"C'mon in my office." Sam opened the double doors that led off the dining room.

As on campus, three enormous monitors sat on a large desk stacked with papers. But here, bookcases filled the opposite wall, and two leather club chairs faced each other opposite the door. It looked like an English gentlemen's club and at the same time, very high tech. Kind of how I envisioned the offices of the top officials at Scotland Yard, only messier, even messier than Sam's office at the university. Apparently, his last-minute tidying had not extended this far.

I tilted my head toward the monitors. "This sure looks a lot different from when it was the card room. At least that's what my family called it. My grandmother had two tables of bridge in here every Wednesday."

"Really?"

"Oh, yes. Before that, I think Great-Great-Grandma Elsie and her mother had meetings of the local Women's Missionary Society here. This is where the hatpin stabbing took place."

Sam's eyes lit up. "The hatpin stabbing? I've got to hear about that."

"Well, okay." Slowly, savoring the story, I told him about the day, back when Elsie was in her teens, that she, her mother, and their friends were discussing how to help a needy area family when a masked man broke in. "He pointed a revolver at the president of the society and demanded that the women hand over their jewelry. While he was threatening the other ladies, Elsie snuck up behind him, pulled out her hatpin, and jabbed him in the arm. That pin was about ten inches long, as thick as a pencil lead, with a mother-of-pearl handle on one end and a sharp point on the other. The robber dropped his revolver, the women attacked him with their umbrellas, and he ended up in jail."

"This was your great-grandmother?"

I held up two fingers. "Two greats. She later served as the mayor of the town for more than two decades. Her diaries are on display at the museum, as is the hatpin."

"Fascinating." He looked around the room, as if envisioning the scene. "Thanks for telling me."

"Happy to. You know historians, always glad to talk about the past." Somehow, I'd enjoyed recounting the tale even more than I expected. Maybe because it wasn't just *hist*ory. This was *my* story, a story I'd probably be telling more in my new job. I hadn't really thought about how nice that connection would be when I took the job in Dogwood Springs.

"Speaking of the past..." Sam opened a tall cabinet along the side wall and pulled out the painting, which was about twenty-four inches by thirty inches and had a thick, gold, ornate wooden frame. The image showed a mother, father, and a girl who looked about thirteen. From the style of the garments, I guessed the year to be about 1900. They stood in a formal parlor and to their left, an open window showed a view of city hall.

I studied the image, and my shoulders sank.

"See?" Sam pointed to the lower right-hand corner of the painting. "That first name is clearly 'Clayton', and the last name starts with an S. The rest is illegible, but I found paintings by Clayton Smithton online, and the signature looks the same."

I peered down at the signature.

Sam continued, his voice filled with excitement. "To me, the style looks like his work. And whoever the family is, they were clearly in Dogwood Springs. The city hall looks the same except that the trees around it are smaller."

That was the problem. "I'm sorry, Sam. That is the Dogwood Springs City Hall, but I can see why Vivian wasn't interested."

"Why?"

"Because this is the new city hall. It's supposed to look old, but it wasn't around when Clayton Smithton was alive. Or when people dressed like this." Before I took the job in Dogwood Springs, I'd had a long talk with my mom about the historic buildings in the area. She'd told me that the original city hall had burned in 1936 and that, for a time, while a new city hall was being built, Elsie had run the town from the attic of the police station. I touched the side of the frame. "Maybe someone painted the family from a photograph, trying to make it look like a Clayton Smithton."

Sam blew out a heavy breath. "I really thought I'd found a treasure. It's weird that it was in the attic here. Did you have any ancestors who were famous art forgers?"

"No. Nobody in my family was artistic at all, at least not that I know of. But—" I leaned in and peered more closely at the window and the image of city hall. "Can we take this where there's more light?"

He looked up quickly. "Sure." He picked up the painting and carried it into the kitchen, then placed it on the enormous island and flipped on all the lights in the room. There were probably surgical suites at the local hospital that had less light.

I leaned down and squinted at the brushwork. "You wouldn't, by any chance, have a magnifying glass, would you?"

He shook his head.

"Well, I may be crazy, but I think Vivian and I might both have been wrong. The brushwork on the window and city hall seems different from the rest of the painting."

"Like—like someone painted over something?"

"Exactly. Which would mean that it really could be a Clayton Smithton underneath."

"Wow." Sam looked over at me, then bent down and studied the painting.

"I'm not sure, of course. Why don't we ask someone from the art department at the university to take a look? They could at least tell us if my theory is correct."

"I'll call over there tomorrow." Sam stood back up. "If they say you're right, I'll find out where to take the painting to have it restored."

"That sounds like a great plan." I stepped toward the living room and picked up my purse. "Thanks for showing me the painting. And the house."

"I appreciate you coming by." He led the way to the front door. "And being so gracious about the house. If it had been built by my family, I don't know that I'd like someone else living in it."

I shrugged. "I'm just glad you're taking such good care of the place." There was no way—no way in the world—I could afford the work that he'd had done on Ashlington. "Besides, I'm quite happy where I am, close to downtown. After commuting in Philly, I love being able to walk to work."

"I can understand that. After I moved here from Silicon Valley, it took me a month to remember that I didn't need to allow forty-five minutes to drive to the grocery store."

Speaking of time, I realized that the sun had fully set, and it had to be after nine. "I should be going. I didn't mean to keep you so long."

"My pleasure." He flipped on the outdoor lights and gave me a warm smile. "As soon as I learn anything about the painting, I'll call you."

Tingles shot through me. "Great." I said goodbye, walked out to my car, and firmly told myself that those tingles were because I was interested in the painting, nothing more.

Chapter Nine

AFTER BREAKFAST ON THURSDAY, since I couldn't do any more work for the museum until I had access to the building, I started a crossword.

Bella, though, had other ideas. She dug a tennis ball out of the edge where the sides met the bottom pillow of her bed, carried it over to me, and dropped it near my feet.

"A subtle hint, huh?" I chuckled, picked up the ball, and walked toward the kitchen door.

Bella wriggled out the door ahead of me and then raced circles around me, eager for the game to begin.

"Okay, girl, here goes." I stood by the driveway in one corner of the yard and threw the ball diagonally across to the farthest corner.

She bounded after it, racing across the grass and catching the ball in the air after it bounced off a chunk of limestone that stuck up above the grass. She spun in midair and raced back to me at top speed, dropping the drool-covered ball at my feet.

Again and again, I tossed the ball for her, and I was struck by how completely she lived in the moment. All those sayings about mindfulness, about letting go of worries —they could have simply said, "live like your dog, playing fetch." This time for her was purely about joy.

How could I spend time out here with her and not feel some of that joy myself?

Eventually, after a bad throw on my part, when I had to get the ball unstuck from a bush at the back of the yard, I promised Bella we'd play fetch again soon and led her inside.

I washed the drool and grass off my hands, then made a serious attempt at unpacking. Bella supervised, lounging on the floor, as I unboxed my turntable and speakers and put on a Steely Dan album. "My Old School" was blasting when Faye, the owner of the bed and breakfast where I'd stayed in April, and a high school friend of my mom's, stopped by to check on me. I turned the music down and assured her that despite finding a dead body, I was fine. She promised to have me over for dinner one day soon, gave me a Dogwood Springs sweatshirt as a welcome-to-town gift, and chatted until ten, when she said she had to dash back to the bed and breakfast.

I watched her drive away and was still at the front window, peering out as it began to rain, when my phone rang.

"Miss Ballard? Detective Harper here. We've finished

gathering evidence at the museum. You can return to the building now."

"Oh, thank you." I put him on speaker and set the phone on a box I still needed to unpack.

"I'm hopeful we'll make an arrest soon, but until then, I'd advise you to keep the museum closed to the public and not to be there alone."

"The board met recently and came to a similar conclusion."

"Good."

If I was going to say anything more, I'd better hurry before he got off the phone. "I, um, I hope you still don't suspect Imani."

Silence. Then he let out a grunt. "For your own safety, I will tell you that Miss Jones continues to be a person of interest."

Seriously? He'd made no progress beyond suspecting Imani? "Really, she looked way too shocked when we found the body to be the killer."

"Miss Ballard, I have a daughter about the same age as Imani. I saw her in several drama club performances when she was in high school. She's quite a good actress. I recommend you be careful."

Could he be right? Could Imani be the killer? No, look at how excited she was showing me the crib her husband was making. Everything about her seemed authentic and, well, just plain nice. I simply couldn't imagine her committing murder.

But I couldn't seem to convince Detective Harper of

that. I crossed my arms over my chest and glared at my phone. Now would be the time to tell him about another possible suspect, if I had one. Which I didn't. "Thank you for letting me know that we can go in the building."

"Just remember, be careful. Whoever killed Vivian is still out there."

"I know." Believe me, I hadn't forgotten about the killer. But was I being careful like the detective said? I had a pretty good idea he wouldn't be happy if he knew I'd talked to Phil yesterday.

On the other hand, the murderer needed to be caught, and the museum needed to reopen, and Detective Harper didn't seem to be making any progress at all in solving the case.

Somehow, I had to figure this mystery out. But first, I needed to hire a locksmith.

I got a recommendation from Alice, made an appointment for half an hour later, and called Rodney and Imani to let them know we had access to the building. While they should still work from home, if they needed anything after the locks were changed, I could let them in to retrieve it. Imani said she had everything she needed to keep her busy, but Rodney said he wanted to work up a proposal for new display cases and would come by while the locksmith was there. I put on my tall rain boots and slicker and walked to the museum.

I'd gone less than a block before I realized that the detective's call didn't only mean the staff could get things we needed for work, it also meant I could take another step in my investigation. I quickly called Cleo and got a number for Zeke.

"Don't bother calling," she said. "He never has his volume on. You'll have to send a text and hope that he sees it."

As it turned out, Zeke replied to my text almost immediately, and he volunteered to ride his bike to the museum and meet me there at eleven. Determination fluttered in my chest, and I picked up my pace, stomping in some shallow puddles simply for the joy of watching them splash. If Zeke could find information on the server from Vivian's emails and calendar, we might have some real clues to work with.

The locksmith, a beefy guy named Brock, was quick and efficient. While he worked on the front door and then the back, I hovered nearby. I tried to wipe smudges of fingerprint powder off the door frames with tissues from my purse, but it didn't all come off. Cleaning this mess was going to be a real pain. There was bound to be a lot more in Vivian's office.

Thinking of Vivian's office reminded me of the bust of Harry Truman. I kicked myself for not bringing it back and told myself to remember it next time. For a moment, I considered going through the museum to see where else the police had left fingerprint powder. But the thought of wandering around alone gave me chills, so I went back to watching Brock work.

Before he left, he volunteered to go through the building with me.

I gratefully accepted, and we locked the front door

behind us. As we walked farther into the front hall, I noticed fingerprint powder on the stair rail.

I pulled a tissue from my purse and made a futile attempt to wipe away the smudge. I was going to need some sort of cleaner. Maybe Murphy's Oil Soap? I'd have to check online. With this mess, even if the killer was arrested today, opening the museum to the public was out of the question. "The curator and I begged them to be careful. I really hope they didn't get fingerprint powder on any of the artifacts."

Brock's eyebrows scrunched down. "I guess all we can do is check."

Room by room, we went through the display space, the gift shop, and the conference room on the first floor, the additional display rooms on the second floor, Imani and Rodney's offices, and the restrooms on each level. We didn't find any intruders, and thankfully, I only found fingerprint powder in the conference room, the hallways, and the stairwells.

I gladly let Brock go alone to check for intruders in Vivian's office, as well as to the basement, where I imagined covens of spiders and their even creepier cousins, centipedes, lurked in the shadows.

While Brock was checking those areas alone, Rodney knocked on the front door. I let him in, and after a trip to his office, he left with a box of papers. Once Brock was finished, I thanked him profusely and promised to post a glowing review of his services online. As I unlocked the front door to let him out, I found that the rain had stopped, only to be replaced by a wave of humidity.

I quickly went back inside and relocked the door. Then I went through the whole building again. I hadn't wanted to slow Brock down earlier, but I'd noticed signs of possible neglect that I needed to look at again. I was beginning to worry the museum hadn't been kept up. Now that I felt safe here, I wanted to check.

I started with the basement. The sooner it was done, the better. After telling myself that centipedes and spiders were more afraid of me than I was of them, I went down the open wooden stairs. I found a single large room with concrete walls and a concrete floor, illuminated by a few lightbulbs in the most basic of ceiling fixtures. There was a crack in one wall, but it had been repaired. Not bad for a building this old. I didn't see a single centipede. And despite the fact that the corners of the ceiling were wispy with cobwebs, I only saw one spider, a big, ugly one with an enormous web near a pallet where someone had stored new member packets.

I gave the spider wide berth and scurried upstairs.

I wouldn't be volunteering to bring up new member packets, but the basement seemed in decent condition. What I found upstairs was less encouraging. Window after window needed weather stripping. In the conference room, the floor sloped slightly toward the back of the house, leaving a gap under the back door that was large enough to let in daylight. And although some of the display cases were museum grade, like the one that held a few gold lockets and some jet beads, other cases, like the one that held Elsie's personal effects, appeared to have been made for a retail store, with no consideration for conservation, environment, or security. The display stand was topped with a simple acrylic cover that did nothing more than keep out the dust. No wonder Rodney was working up a proposal.

From the looks of the rest of the museum, I'd guess he'd made it before. I remembered Imani mentioning that Vivian hadn't liked to spend money on tech. That cheap attitude seemed to have extended to other items as well, items that were essential to protecting the artifacts we had been entrusted with. I finished my exploration, making notes on my phone as I stopped in each room. All of this would have to be discussed at the next board meeting and—

My phone dinged with a text from Zeke, who was waiting outside.

I let him in, relocked the front door, and led the way to Vivian's office. At the door, I hesitated, wishing I'd gone inside with Brock. "I don't really know how bad things are going to be in here. Are you okay going in? And would your mom be okay with it?"

He raised his eyebrows. "Seriously? I'm expecting some dried blood, maybe a hole in the plaster where they dug out a slug. Pretty tame compared to Call of Duty."

"That's a video game. This is real."

"Don't worry. You're not going to give me nightmares. Unless you make me give a presentation in class."

I laughed. "Well, all right." I opened the door.

Vivian's office, which I guess was now mine, had gotten the full force of the forensic team. Papers that I vaguely remembered seeing stacked were in disarray, and finger-print powder was everywhere.

I walked closer to the desk but quickly pulled my foot back from where my toes had landed under the edge of the desk. My flats were cute, but the soles were thin enough that I knew I'd stepped on something. I leaned down, peered under the desk, and picked up a wood chip about half an inch long and a quarter of an inch thick. Wait, had the desk been damaged in the murder? No, the chip was too light in color to have come from the desk. It was more the color of the crib Dale was building. Perhaps the chip had gotten snagged on Imani's sweater and fallen off when we found Vivian's body. I dropped it in my purse and forced myself to walk around to the back of the desk.

A chunk of the upholstery of the desk chair had been cut out, and I could only guess that the police might have dug out a bullet. I shuddered. I was definitely ordering a new chair. Thankfully, there was less blood than I'd imag-ined. Maybe Vivian's heart had stopped immediately. For her sake, I hoped so. "Let's look in the file cabinet, take anything that seems related to the computer system, and get out of here."

Zeke, for all his earlier bluster, readily agreed.

I dug a large file folder labeled "Computer Stuff" out of a drawer. "Why don't we go over to my apartment to work?"

"What about lunch?"

I checked my phone. It was only eleven fifteen, but I remembered my brother as a teenager. After a brief discus-sion, I pulled out my wallet and handed Zeke a twenty.

"Thanks." He slid it in his pocket. His favorite sub shop was in the opposite direction of my apartment but, motivated by the offer of free food, he was willing to ride over and pick up our order.

I told Zeke I'd meet him at my apartment after an errand. I was walking out of Vivian's office when the cordless phone on the desk rang. I grabbed the receiver and followed Zeke downstairs.

"Hello? This is Libby Ballard." I locked the front door behind Zeke and started back up the stairs.

"Patricia Webb here. Are you the new director Vivian told me about?"

"I am." I didn't know the names of all the donors to the museum, but I knew hers. Other than the trust fund, she was the biggest donor. "So nice to talk with you, Mrs. Webb," I lied. Actually, I'd much rather have had time to prepare something to say. On paper. "Vivian spoke highly of you. How can I help you?"

"Please, call me Patricia. I wondered if you or someone affiliated with the museum might know someone I can talk with at the police station besides Detective Harper. I called over there earlier today, thinking I had information that could potentially help the police find the person who killed Vivian, but no one has called me back."

"I'm so sorry." I glanced at the hole in the chair that had been Vivian's, then sat in the straight-backed guest chair. "I think he's the person you need to speak with. Hopefully, he'll return your call soon." I hesitated, trying to think of a way to get her to share her information with me. "Patricia, I know this may seem odd, but I can't help but want this resolved for Vivian's sake and for the sake of the staff here at the museum. Did Vivian indicate to you that she felt she was in danger here in the building?"

"Oh, no, nothing like that. It was who I saw her having dinner with."

She proceeded to tell me about an evening about a month ago when she had been eating dinner with a friend at an upscale restaurant in Jefferson City. "It's a fabulous place, delicious Italian food," she said. While Patricia was there, she saw Vivian looking "very chummy" with a man who Patricia knew wasn't Vivian's husband. "When they were leaving, Vivian acted as if she wanted to introduce me, but the man glared at her and practically yanked her out of the dining room."

Excitement rose in my chest. This guy did sound like a good suspect. "What did he look like?"

"It's been so long that all I remember is that he had brown hair. But I think I'd recognize him if I saw him. And I know the dinner was the night of May fifth."

"Hmmm." My excitement faded. "A lot of men have brown hair, so I'm not sure how the police will find the right one. But the fact that Vivian may have been having an affair is a really good clue, especially if her divorce wasn't final and her husband didn't know about the affair."

"Well, I thought so. I hope Detective Harper calls back soon."

"Me too. It was smart of you to think of it."

"Thank you, dear," she said warmly. "My grandchildren

live there in Dogwood Springs, and I do enjoy supporting the museum so they have a place right there in town where they can learn about history. It's much more likely to capture their attention than a lesson from a book. But"— she let out a heavy sigh—"I don't feel responsible contributing to the museum when I don't think they'd be safe there."

I gulped. Exactly what I'd been afraid of. If Patricia felt this way, other donors were bound to feel the same. "Don't worry. I'm sure the criminal will be caught, and the Dogwood Springs History Museum will soon be reopened, ready to delight your grandchildren and others with the rich history of the area."

"I hope so. I mean, I guess I could give the money I have earmarked for the museum to other charities. My accountant seems eager for me to disperse some funds for tax purposes."

My stomach clenched. No! That would be horrible! Not just because of how it might affect my job, but because people from all walks of life and from all sorts of places, even little towns like Dogwood Springs, needed access to cultural history and arts. "I... I know there are so many worthy causes today, but I really hope you'll hang on for a little longer until the situation here at the museum can be resolved." My mind raced. How could I entice her? "I have some wonderful plans for future exhibits that I was hoping to get your opinion on."

"Oh, that would be nice. Vivian never asked my opinion, and I do have some ideas about what children might enjoy."

My stomach eased, at least partly. "Exactly the feedback I was hoping you might provide. Shall we make an appointment, say in two weeks? I'm sure the museum will be back to normal by then."

She agreed, and we set a date and time for me to drive to Jefferson City to meet with her.

Two weeks.

Surely, it would be enough time for me to come up with those plans for future exhibits for us to discuss.

And enough time for me to solve this case.

I dropped a set of the new keys with Alice, hurried home, and just had time to let Bella out for a few minutes and put out fresh water and some kibble for her lunch before Zeke arrived.

Bella ate, took a big slurp of water, and then flopped by the couch while Zeke and I gobbled down our lunch.

From the size of the bites Zeke took, I had a feeling he gobbled down every meal. For my part, I ate quickly because Miller's subs were indeed delicious and because I was eager to see if there was any information in the computer files—maybe a note in Vivian's calendar on May 5?—that would help us identify the man Patricia saw her with.

While we ate, Zeke and I flipped through the material from the manila folder from Vivian's files, but we didn't find anything useful. I didn't expect a nice, neat list of passwords, but I'd hoped for more than a stack of receipts and a software manual printed in 1998.

"How are we ever going to get into the museum's account on the server without the password?" I wadded up the trash from our lunch and shoved it back in the bag. "Do you think I should call Imani? Maybe she would know?"

"Give me a minute." Zeke glanced back down at something on one of the receipts and pulled his laptop out of his backpack. His fingers flew over the keyboard, and a second later, a grin spread across his face. "Got it."

My hands fell to my sides. "You're kidding? What was the password?

"I'm sure the service provider gave her a decent password when they set things up, but since it was for the admin account, someone cleverly changed it to 'admin.'" He rolled his eyes. "People are so stupid."

I said nothing and silently vowed to myself to change some of my personal passwords. I wasn't sure, but I had a feeling that my Netflix password was "movies." I stepped to where I could look over Zeke's shoulder. "Uh, so what do you see?"

"Well, Vivian's electronic calendar, her email, and a folder of stuff she uploaded to the cloud."

My heart picked up speed. "Let's look at her calendar first." I pulled up a chair next to him. "Early May."

Zeke tapped the keyboard a couple times, then turned the laptop so I could better see the screen.

He clicked to May, and my heart sank.

There were no appointments on May 5.

We looked back as far as the first of the year but found nothing that jumped out as a clue.

Oh, sure, there were lots of meetings indicated by initials that we quickly identified as Imani or Rodney, a few meetings with Alice or another board member, which all had a note about a work-related topic, and the monthly board meetings. We found Vivian's monthly hair and nail appointments, always scheduled over her lunch hour, and an appointment in April for the doctor.

The only item we couldn't identify was a note, no time listed, the morning she was murdered, that said H.S.T. But even though I went through every board member and every name on a potential donor list Zeke opened, we found no names that matched the initials H.S.T. Perhaps there was a Historical Society of Tampa that Vivian would have worked with in her new job?

I turned to Zeke. "So much for the calendar. Can we see the stuff she most recently uploaded?"

"Sure." He pulled up a list.

"Ooh." I pointed at a file titled "Things to Discuss with Libby." "Open that."

He did, and I pulled the laptop toward me, scrolling quickly down the document.

In a neat, organized fashion, Vivian had listed the various tasks she handled at the museum, approximate hours she spent weekly on each, and key contacts for maintenance, including a repair service for the HVAC system, which apparently was on its last legs. In addition, she summarized her work on a grant proposal that was due next week.

Next week? I knew what I'd be doing after Zeke left.

"Anything?" Zeke looked over at me.

"Useful stuff for my job, but nothing that helps me figure out who might have killed her."

"Let me look."

I slid the laptop back toward him. He closed the file I'd been reading and scrolled down. "What about this? Every other folder has a name like Development, Staffing ... some business thing. This one's named Madoff."

"As in Bernie Madoff?" I leaned in closer. "The embezzler?"

Zeke clicked the file open.

Sure enough, in the document, Vivian outlined evidence she had found that over the past three years, more than fifty thousand dollars had been embezzled from the museum.

By Dwight, the board treasurer.

And when we looked back at her electronic calendar, we found that he'd had an appointment with Vivian the day before the murder where she planned to discuss the accounts.

I needed to work on that grant proposal, but first it was time for me to have a chat with Detective Harper.

Chapter Ten

MY CONVERSATION with the detective didn't go exactly as I'd hoped. I mean, I didn't actually see steam come out his ears and encircle the stuffed, mounted fish that decorated his beige office, but from the set of his jaw, I wouldn't have been surprised if I had.

He hunched over his desk, elbows out to the sides, and glared at me. "We've already seen everything on Vivian's laptop, and we are pursuing appropriate inquiries. I will send an officer by to get a full statement from you about the embezzlement on behalf of the museum, but you do understand that someone was murdered, don't you?"

My chin instinctively jutted out. "Of course I do. It happened in my office, in the museum that I'm supposed to be the director of but can't open."

"Please, Miss Ballard, stay out of this. Give us time to build a solid case. Isn't there something you can do at the museum, like dust the antiques?"

Dust the antiques?

My cheeks flamed, and my spine went rigid. The items on display at the museum weren't simply *antiques*, they were valuable *artifacts*, telling the history of the town that he, as a police officer, was supposed to care about.

And he wasn't paying attention to a word I was saying. I glared at him. "Are you listening? Dwight was stealing money from the museum, and he met with Vivian the day before she was murdered."

"I know that. And I knew that before you waltzed in here."

"Then why aren't you arresti—"

"Miss Ballard, don't tell me how to do my job." He stood. "I've learned who you are, and if you're as headstrong as your mother, I realize I may be wasting my breath. But I'll say it anyway. Go home. Stop playing detective. Even though your mom and I weren't the best of friends in high school, I don't want to have to tell her that her daughter's been murdered."

My stomach bunched into a tight ball.

I really didn't want that either.

I grabbed my purse, yanked it onto my shoulder, and left with as much dignity as I could muster.

"John Harper's a good guy." My mother sounded as if she'd been fonder of him than he of her. "But Faye says people have been leaving the Dogwood Springs Police Department for positions in bigger towns where the pay is better. And then his brother had that heart attack. She says John's nearly run ragged. Why don't you come stay with Dad and me here in Columbus, Libby, until this situation gets resolved?"

"I can't come home, Mom." I sprawled on my living room couch and propped my feet on a box of memorabilia I still needed to unpack. "I'm the director. I'm supposed to provide leadership to the museum staff and board. I don't think running out of town is providing leadership, do you?"

That silenced her, at least temporarily.

Bella laid her head on my thigh.

I ran my fingers over her velvety ears and exhaled, dissipating some of my frustration.

"I still don't like the idea of you being in danger." My mother sniffed. "And I can't believe I had to hear the details from Faye. Your dad just glossed over everything as if it was fine. You should have called me and told me that the person who previously had your job had been murdered. And right in what will be your office, according to Faye."

A knot of guilt tightened in my chest. She was right. I should have called her. Not calling Monday, the day of the murder, was excusable. But sometime yesterday or the day before, I should have told her more about what happened. I could only imagine Faye, calling to say she'd checked on me and I was fine, and my mom being clueless of the details.

I pressed my lips together. "I'm sorry. I didn't want to upset you, Mom. Maybe the chief of police will be better soon and be back on the job." There. That was something we both could hope for.

"According to Faye, that heart attack nearly killed him. He's not expected back at work for a month."

Oh. Well, that was depressing. "But what does John Harper have against you, Mom? Something that happened in high school?"

No answer.

"Mom?"

"It really wasn't a big deal. You'd think he'd be over it by now."

"Be over what?"

Mom let out a sigh. "He wanted to date a friend of mine and came to me for advice. I was trying to save him from embarrassment. I mean, never in a million years was she going to date him, but I may not have handled it as diplomatically as I should have. And, well, you know male pride."

"You insulted him. Thanks a lot, Mom."

"It wasn't like I had any idea you were going to take a job in Dogwood Springs when I was in high school. You weren't even born."

"True." But I could easily imagine the scene. My mother was a talk-first, think-later, not-as-well-filtered-as-she-should-be kind of person. And being her daughter in this situation wasn't helping me a bit. "I'll check in with you later."

"For heaven's sake, be careful, Libby. John's right. This is no time to play Nancy Drew."

"Love you, Mom." I hung up.

No time to play Nancy Drew? I scowled at my phone. I'd always been fond of those books, and good old Nancy had solved a lot of cases. Besides, I had every intention of being careful, but I couldn't sit idly by. If the chief of police wasn't coming back for a month, and if John Harper was as overworked as my mother said, it could be weeks before the murderer was caught.

Weeks!

No amount of fast talking and schmoozing would help me win Patricia's donation then. The museum would be in serious financial straits, especially since Dwight had stolen any reserve cash the non-profit had. I might have to lay off staff.

Or I might find myself out of a job.

I had been frustrated enough by my visit to the police station, but I felt even worse after an officer came by my apartment to take a statement about the embezzling. He admitted that the police had no hard evidence that Dwight had killed Vivian. Motive, yes. Opportunity, yes, but no solid evidence to tie him to the killing.

After he left, I poured myself a glass of iced tea and sank onto my couch. Somehow, some way, I needed evidence that Detective Harper hadn't found, evidence that would prove Dwight was the killer.

But how to find it?

I tapped one finger on my cheekbone, thinking.

Finally, just as Cleo's Jeep drove past the front of the house and turned in the drive, I had an idea.

I scrambled off the couch and caught her as she headed up the stairs to her apartment, carrying two large bags from the local craft store.

"Small addiction," she said, raising the bags. "I can stop anytime I want."

I brushed the comment aside. I wasn't ever giving up my crosswords, so I'd be the last one to criticize her for buying too many craft supplies. "Remember when you offered to go with me when I confronted a possible killer?"

Her eyes lit. "I do."

"I'm going to take you up on that."

Half an hour later, after brainstorming in my living room, Cleo and I had a plan. Tomorrow morning, after she made an early trip to the post office and before she opened the salon, we'd meet at the CPA firm at nine. Once we were in Dwight's office, she would pretend to be replying to a text but in truth would be starting the voice recorder on her phone. Then I would flat out accuse Dwight of embezzlement and murder.

If we were lucky, he'd say enough that the recording would convince the detective.

"This seems like a long shot. The police must have already questioned him." Cleo pulled her feet up, sitting cross-legged on the couch.

"I know. But he'd have been really cautious talking to the police. Maybe we can catch him unaware."

~

As soon as I entered the lobby of the CPA firm the next morning, I realized I should have texted Cleo first. She was nowhere to be seen, and the receptionist was looking at me expectantly.

I stepped up to the window. "I, uh, I'm here to see Dwight, but I—"

"No need to worry about an appointment. I remember you from the other day when you came to see Phil." She gestured to the door to the hall that led to the offices. "Go ahead on back. Dwight's the last door on the right. Knock and then go right on in. He's on the phone, but he's been on that call forever. I know he'll welcome the excuse to escape."

The phone on her desk rang, and she looked at me, then at the door that led from the lobby to the offices in the back.

Definitely awkward. Where was Cleo? It had to be well after nine. "Please send my friend Cleo back when she arrives." I went into the back hall, giving myself a pep-talk as I walked.

No need to confront Dwight right away. No need to say anything about the murder until Cleo got here. No need to act nervous.

But no more stalling out here in the hall. Surely, I could make small talk until Cleo arrived. Dwight was on the board, so I could always ask how he thought we should handle the reopening. If nothing else, I could ask what was wrong with their air-conditioner, which had just kicked on. Here toward the back of the building, it sounded like a plane taking off.

The door on the right was ajar. "Dwight?" I edged it open slightly.

And backed away with my eyes squeezed shut.

A scream that might have been mine echoed through the hall, even louder than the air-conditioner.

Because there was no way I was going to get Dwight Bower to confess to murdering Vivian.

I took another quick peek.

Things hadn't improved.

Dwight sat upright in his chair, but his head hung limp. Purplish-red bruises encircled his neck, just above the collar of his pale blue polo shirt. The phone receiver lay on the desk where he'd apparently dropped it, a busy signal buzzing out.

I'd discovered my second dead body in less than a week.

Chapter Eleven

TO SAY that Detective Harper was a little upset with me was like saying that Bella was a little friendly. He jabbed a finger toward the accounting firm's conference room, glared at me until I walked there and sat down at the long cherry table, then told a female officer not to take her eyes off me.

He spun and was almost out the door of the room when he stopped and turned back. "You are all right, aren't you? Not faint or anything?"

"I'm fine." A little water would be nice, but I wasn't about to ask.

I let out a shaky breath as Phil, a woman in a business suit who I assumed was the other CPA, and the office staff joined us. Two men and a woman then came in, probably other clients from the way Phil and the office staff responded.

The police officer assured us that the detective would

speak with us as quickly as possible and instructed us not to talk while we waited.

The other CPA gave the rest of us a jerky nod, took a chair in a back corner, and proceeded to pick off all her fingernail polish without saying a word.

The three clients, who seemed to know each other, took chairs together in a corner near the door. At first, one of the men typed notes to the others on his phone, holding it out for them to read, until the police officer told them to stop communicating.

The two women I'd seen in the front office huddled side by side at the far end of the table. Occasionally, as if unable to contain herself, one of them whispered to the other, loud enough that I overheard things like "serial killer" and "who's next?"

Phil sat across from me, at the end of the table near the door, rubbing the collar of his dress shirt, looking dazed. A perfectly reasonable reaction, but all I could think of was the fact that it could all be an act. He could easily have slipped into Dwight's office and killed him. And here I was, six feet away from him, the stranger in town who'd stopped by for that awkward conversation the other day. He hadn't seemed guilty, but I didn't know him, so who was I to judge? No matter how friendly he seemed when he talked about that dachshund, he and Vivian were in the middle of a bitter divorce, and he was the beneficiary of her life insurance policy. Motive heaped upon motive.

But why would he kill Dwight at the office where they

both worked? I glanced over at Phil, trying to come up with a scenario where that made sense.

He looked up at me, as if he'd felt my gaze.

The last thing I wanted to do was make it even more obvious that I suspected him, so I gave what I hoped looked like a nervous, we're-all-in-this-together smile. To avoid further conversation, I took out my little notebook and made a list of potential displays for the museum, trying to appear focused on my task and not glance repeatedly at the female police officer for reassurance that I was safe.

My phone dinged with a text and everyone in the room looked at me.

I silenced it and read a message from a frantic Cleo, who apologized profusely for being delayed at the post office. She'd heard there were police at the CPA's office and wanted to make sure I was safe.

After asking the officer's permission, I responded and assured Cleo that I was fine. Nervous, but fine.

She replied with a wide-eyed emoji, a shame-faced emoji, and another apology.

Finally, after more than an hour, Harper called me out of the conference room and took me to Phil's office, which he had apparently chosen as his interview room. Harper took my statement, tension lacing every question. Finally, he stopped and looked over at me.

"You, Miss Ballard, are extremely lucky that you haven't gotten yourself killed." He stared at me, nostrils flaring, dark, bushy eyebrows almost joined. "We've had two murders in the past week, and in each case, you seem to have arrived on the scene only minutes after the crime occurred."

"That's a little unfair. How was I to know that Vivian had been murdered right before I was supposed to start my first day working at the museum?"

He leaned back in the cushy desk chair and pursed his lips. "And today? One day after you tell me that you think Dwight is the killer, and I tell you to stay out of the investigation, you just happen to stop by to see him?"

My gaze sank to the floor, and I shrank down in my chair. Still not ready to meet the detective's eyes, I looked over at the credenza and studied the picture of Oscar, Phil and Vivian's black dachshund.

"I have half a mind to lock you up for your own safety." Harper let out a snort. "Wouldn't that be priceless? One of the esteemed Dorsett family behind bars?"

"But you don't have any evidence against me! How could you—"

"I didn't say I was going to. As you'll see in a few minutes, we're taking Phil in for further questioning."

"He killed her for the life insurance, right?"

Harper glared at me and stood. "I'm sure I'll learn more when I question him. In the meantime, I want you—in fact I order you—to leave this case alone." He jerked a thumb toward the door. "If I find out you're doing anything further related to this case, I'll arrest you for interfering with a police investigation and put you in a cell."

~

Finally, four hours after I'd arrived at the CPA firm, Phil was taken to the station, and the rest of us were allowed to go home.

I hurried home, let Bella out, and then sat on the concrete steps by my kitchen door, soaking in the sunshine and petting her, trying to feel calmer.

Even Bella's presence and affection couldn't ease the tension in my neck and shoulders. I sat there, getting more and more nervous as images of Dwight and Vivian's bodies flashed through my mind. What if the police didn't have enough evidence to hold Phil and he came after me because I'd put myself in the middle of this with my snooping?

Finally, I stood up. "Bella? How would you feel about a walk?"

She let out a happy bark, and I took her inside so I could change into shorts and tennis shoes and get her leash. Five minutes later, we were back outside. Already, I felt better. At least I wasn't simply sitting there worrying.

I started to take Bella on a new route, down Fifth Street, but Bella angled her head at me, her big brown eyes confused.

"All right. Phil is at the police station. I guess it's safe to go past his house."

She trotted ahead on our usual route.

The walk was good for me. The day was hot but not oppressively so. And there was something healing about seeing the beautiful flowers in every yard, hearing the birds twittering in the trees and—in the spaces between those trees—feeling the sun warming my arms.

At first, when we approached Phil's house, I kept my eyes focused on the sidewalk ahead. When we reached his mailbox, though, I couldn't resist a quick peek at the house.

Suddenly, Bella yanked the leash free from my hand and bolted across Phil's yard.

"Bella! Come back here."

She ignored me.

With no other alternative, I dashed after her.

By the time I caught up with her, she was around the side of the house, hidden from the road by a large lilac bush, and barking loudly.

She sniffed at the flowerbed beside the house and stuck her nose into some fresh mulch spread around a clump of day lilies. Sniffed and barked and—

"Bella! No!" I ran toward her. "Stop digging right this min—"

I looked down at what she'd dug up.

And my skin went tingly.

"Bella!" My heart pounded as I grabbed her collar and pulled her away from the house, toward the street.

Away from the towel she had pulled out from under the mulch.

And away from the gun that tumbled out.

Adrenaline shot through my veins, but I hurriedly brushed the mulch off Bella's nose and paws and—just in case Phil Martin happened to be driving home—did my best to walk nonchalantly toward my apartment, trying to look as if I'd never seen a murder weapon in his side yard.

After I was inside my apartment with the doors locked, I heaved out a sigh and called the police.

An hour later, through my living room window, I saw Detective Harper walk up my sidewalk, then I heard a knock on the outside front door.

I glanced over at Bella. "If you're all alone tonight because I'm locked in jail for interfering with a police investigation, it's your own fault."

She looked up from where she lay in front of the fireplace, grinned at me, and flopped her tail rhythmically on the floor.

I opened the door to my apartment, then the main door to the outside.

"Miss Ballard!" Detective Harper bellowed, eyebrows bristling. "I—

"It wasn't me. It was Bella." I let him in, gestured for him to sit on my couch, and pointed at my four-legged friend.

Harper tipped his head to one side, and his anger seemed to subside. "Bella?" he asked in a normal voice.

I nodded.

He sat down on one end of the couch. I took the other. As if on cue, Bella walked over and licked his hand.

He rubbed the dog's ears. "I know this is Don Felding's old apartment. Did you adopt his dog too?"

"I did," I answered slowly. I'd been expecting the detective to read me the riot act, not ask details about my dog.

"Um, Bella seemed to be attached to this place and kept turning up. She wasn't happy living with Mr. Felding's daughter because she was never home. Plus," I shrugged, "I thought it would be nice to have a pet. I recently went through an ugly divorce."

Detective Harper's eyes narrowed, and he gazed down at Bella for a long moment, then back up at me. His shoulders relaxed and what I'd swear was sympathy softened his eyes. "I can understand that. Tell me what happened at Phil Martin's house."

I explained that I had taken Bella on our usual walk, admitting that I knew I'd be passing Phil's house. "I thought it would be okay, though, since I figured he was still at the police station. And then Bella just got away from me. I really don't understand it. She usually stays right by my side. But she ran straight toward Phil's house and around to the side yard, like maybe she smelled the new mulch or maybe an animal."

"New mulch?"

"Well, it looked new to me. Even where Bella didn't dig, it was all fluffed up, not matted down."

"Maybe you're right. Maybe it was the mulch. Or an animal." Harper angled his head and looked at Bella again. "But Don Felding always did say he had the smartest dog in town."

I sat there, blinking, putting together what had happened with what Harper said. "Really?" Bella understood a lot of words, but... "You mean you think ... you think she knew the gun was there?"

Harper spread his hands wide, as if to say *who knows?* "I'm not putting it in my report, that's for sure."

I felt my mouth drop open, then words tumbled out. "Do you think she was a police dog? Like she was trained to sniff out firearms?"

"Don never said that, and I think he would have mentioned it. He just said that she was really smart." He gave Bella a pat and stood up. "Anyway, I'm glad that, for once, you weren't trying to investigate. For now, we've kept Phil at the station, and we'll be testing the gun for prints and gun-shot residue."

I walked with him toward the door with Bella at my side.

In the entryway, he stopped and turned to me. "I don't know how long we can hold Phil, so I'm telling you what I'd tell my own daughter. Until this case is solved, Libby, take your walks in another direction." He took one last look at Bella and headed out the door.

I sat back down on the couch, staring at Bella. "Full of surprises, aren't you girl? I mean I knew you were helping me meet people here in Dogwood Springs, but who knew that you—and my divorce—would help me get on better terms with Detective Harper? And who knew you were so smart?"

Bella ambled over, wagged her tail, and looked up at me with a gleam in her eye.

Chapter Twelve

MY MIND REELING, I called Alice and Cleo and texted Zeke and invited them over to share a pizza for dinner and hear the latest news about the case—and about Bella.

By six fifteen, everyone had arrived. Bella met each person, including the pizza delivery girl, like a long-lost friend. Cleo brought down two folding chairs from her apartment. With those, the couch, and a makeshift coffee table I'd constructed by taping together two empty boxes, we sat down in a big circle, just like a family. I even brought in Bella's food bowl so she could join us and added a dog biscuit to her meal as a treat.

"Is it true?" Alice said, settling into the couch. "They arrested Phil? And Bella found a gun in his yard?"

"I don't know if Phil has been formally charged, only that the police were holding him while they tested the gun." I passed out plates and paper napkins and explained what the detective had said. "I knew Bella was smart, but I didn't know she could find clues."

Hearing me say her name, Bella rubbed her head against my leg, and I stroked her back.

"Wow. Bella, you're even more awesome than I thought." Zeke called her over and rubbed her ears.

"Amazing." Cleo helped herself to a slice of pizza. "So, we were right about the motive for Vivian's murder being the insurance money?"

"Apparently," I said.

"It does make sense." Zeke gave Bella a final pat, then grabbed a large slice and folded it in half lengthwise, cheese to cheese. "The story about being at an audit seemed pretty thin." He took a huge bite.

"And impossible to verify, at least for us," I said.

"The police could make Phil divulge who he was with, even if it was confidential." Alice picked up a smaller piece of pizza.

She was right. And the more I thought about things, the more the knots of tension eased in my shoulders. Detective Harper had started off on the wrong track, suspecting Imani, but he could make this case stick. Before we knew it, Phil would be in prison, the museum could reopen, and everyone in Dogwood Springs, including me, could relax.

Then I had another thought. "You know, if Phil somehow knew what Vivian had found out about Dwight's embezzlement, then that actually gives him another motive for killing her." I set my plate on the cardboard coffee table and wiped the grease off my fingers with my napkin.

"Dwight's arrest would have been really bad publicity for the CPA firm. Nobody wants their taxes done by a firm that employed an embezzler."

"Wow." Cleo sat back in her chair, plate on her lap. "From what I heard, that divorce was pretty bitter. And Vivian..." She made a face. "Well, I can imagine her taking a good deal of pleasure in making sure Phil's employer went out of business so he'd lose his job."

I inwardly winced. To be honest, I, too, would find some pleasure in my ex losing his position at the Henry C. Branch House. But only because he'd finagled things so my own position had been eliminated.

"The one thing I don't understand," Cleo said, "is why Phil would have killed Dwight at work. A murder at the CPA firm isn't going to help business."

"Ahh, I've thought about that." I leaned forward, eager to discuss something other than divorce. "Dwight must have seen something that made him suspect Phil, and he confronted him."

Cleo tipped her head to one side. "I guess," she said slowly. "I still think it would have been smarter to kill Dwight somewhere else. And it's been four days since Vivian was killed. Why wouldn't he have gotten rid of the gun?"

Zeke grabbed his third slice of pizza. "If it was me, I'd throw it in Dogwood Springs. That pool is so deep that the gun would never be found."

Alice wiped her mouth and set her napkin beside her plate on the cardboard coffee table. "We may never know all that went on in Phil's head. But I keep thinking of his sister. Would you mind if I went in your kitchen and gave her a call?"

"No. Go right ahead." I hadn't even known Phil had a sister.

"We volunteer at the library together." Alice stood and stepped toward the kitchen. "I'm sure she won't pick up, but I want to leave a message, so she knows I'm thinking of her. This has to be horrible for the whole family."

Zeke, Cleo, and I sat silently for a moment after she left. I'd been so excited that the murder was solved that I hadn't really thought about how it would affect other people. I turned to Cleo. "I wonder what will happen to Dwight's wife." Not only was the poor woman now a widow, but the fact that Dwight had been an embezzler would eventually come out, possibly making people think she was as dishonest as him.

"Her friends and employees have pitched in to run the bakery for a while," Cleo said.

I grimaced. "I bet that ends fast when they learn about Dwight being an embezzler."

"No," Cleo said. "People already know. I don't think anyone blames Jackie for that. I think people are being really supportive."

Humph. That was not what I expected. I took a bite of my pizza and chewed. I still wasn't used to how people thought in a small town.

"You're not going to believe this." Alice rushed back into

the living room. "Phil's been released. His sister said he had an airtight alibi for the time of Vivian's murder."

Cleo, Zeke, and I turned to face her.

"He wasn't at an audit. He only said that because he was too embarrassed to tell you the truth, Libby." She sat back down on the couch and looked at each of us, as if savoring the spotlight. "He was in Columbia having cataract surgery."

"Surgery? Why didn't he say so?"

"He didn't want people to know because he thought having cataracts made him sound old. But he'd far rather admit that than go to jail for murder."

Cleo held up a hand. "Wait. What about the gun?"

"The police think it was planted. It looks like the murder weapon, but it had been wiped clean of prints."

"Not good." Zeke rocked back in his chair. "That means they have no idea who killed Vivian or Dwight."

The tension in my shoulders ratcheted back up. "And neither do we."

The four of us looked at each other.

"What do we do now?" Cleo said.

I set down my pizza, no longer interested in eating. "I don't know, but whatever it is, we do it carefully. Gossip travels so fast in this town that whoever the murderer is, they probably know we're trying to figure this out."

After Alice's news, not even Zeke was interested in pizza. Alice offered to drive him home, saving Cleo the trip, and my housemate went upstairs. I stuck the leftover pizza in the fridge, cleaned up the living room, and—after sliding some pepper spray that I'd bought when I lived in Philly into my pocket—I took Bella out for a quick trip to the backyard.

Eventually, I got ready for bed, but I couldn't sleep. My tossing and turning even kept Bella awake. At about three, I drifted off, only to wake at six in the middle of a nightmare that I was being chased by someone I couldn't recognize.

What a mess.

At first, I admit, I'd made the move to Dogwood Springs reluctantly. Pride, I guess, made me believe I was meant for a better position than director of the Dogwood Springs History Museum.

In less than a week, though, and in spite of two murders, the town had begun to grow on me. Partly, that was Bella. But I also loved walking everywhere, and although I hadn't seen the whole state, I could easily believe Dogwood Springs was the prettiest town in Missouri. More importantly, I really liked the people. Cleo and Alice and even Zeke had accepted me so quickly. In many ways, their friendship felt more authentic than some of the friends I'd had back in Philadelphia, especially the ones who seemed to forget me once Reggie and I divorced. Even people I met here casually seemed friendlier.

I wanted the chance to build a new life here, working at

the museum. And Vivian may not have been the nicest person, but her killer should be brought to justice.

But with no remaining clues to follow up, and with the warnings of John Harper and my mother echoing in my head, I decided that my weekend would best be spent setting up my new apartment. I had to think positively and believe that one day the museum would reopen.

So, on Saturday, I unpacked the last of my boxes and made a trip to Jefferson City to buy some under-bed storage containers, as well as a small dining table for the end of my living room closest to the kitchen. An inexpensive lamp for my nightstand, a new bathmat, and a tiny shelving unit for the bathroom rounded out my purchases and made my new place much more livable.

I couldn't take Bella on my shopping trip, but I stopped at a pet store in Jefferson City and bought her a bouncy toy that I could hide a treat in. Once I got home and unloaded, I gave her a good brushing, then let her play with her new toy. It was a big hit.

By late Sunday, I was completely settled in the new apartment, and the feeling of constant danger had eased. After lunch, Bella and I had another great game of fetch in the backyard. I even started aiming for the exposed chunk of limestone, trying to get the ball to bounce so Bella could catch it in the air, which she loved. After a while, though, the heat and humidity got to both of us, and we went inside. I was working a crossword, listening to the Eagles *Hotel California* album, when the phone rang.

The number was local and seemed familiar.

"Libby? This is Melinda Felding. I wanted to give you a full week before asking how things were working out with Bella. Do you want me to come pick her up?"

I wrapped a protective arm around Bella, who was sitting at my side. "Oh, no. If it's all right with you, I'd love to keep her. I'm enjoying spending time with her, and she seems quite happy here." How could I possibly want to give up the smartest, most loving dog in town? And such a skilled fetch player?

"That's fabulous." Melinda's relief rang out over the phone line. "I could tell by how you interacted with her that you'd take great care of her. I'm so glad it worked out."

"Definitely. I can't really imagine life without her at this point." Warmth swirled around my heart, and I looked down at Bella, who gazed back at me with love.

"Well, I hope the two of you are very happy together," Melinda said.

"I know we will be. Thank you for letting me keep her."

"No, thank you for giving her a home. I know Dad would be pleased." Melinda wished me luck as a pet owner and hung up.

I went into the kitchen and picked up Bella's leash. "Ready for a nice, long walk, girl?"

She let out an excited *woof* and galloped toward the front door. *Walk* was definitely part of her vocabulary.

I rubbed her ears and clipped on the leash, savoring the fact that Bella was mine. Of all the apartments in Dogwood Springs, I'd somehow picked the one that led me to her, and I couldn't be more grateful. Cleo had been out of town for a cousin's wedding, and even though I'd been alone all weekend except for when I went shopping, I hadn't been lonely at all. I gave Bella one last pat and opened the door.

Half a block down Elm, Bella trotted up to an older man, who greeted her by name.

I introduced myself and learned he was a retired English professor named Alan Melkins.

I'd just said hello and explained that I'd moved to town to work at the museum when Bella barked loudly and pulled at the end of the leash.

I tugged her back. "Hush, girl. You need to leave that squirrel alone."

She barked once more and let out a soft whine, her feet planted, eyes still focused on the squirrel.

I shot Professor Melkins an apologetic glance. "Sorry about that. Normally, she's so well behaved."

"I've seen her get excited about squirrels many times when she was out walking with Don Felding. Apparently, she has a special animosity toward them." He shrugged. "But about the museum. Are you going into the building these days? It seems dangerous."

"I've only gone in once after the day Vivian was killed. And I was with someone else." I gave Bella's leash a gentle jerk, and she finally left her position beneath the tree that held the squirrel.

"Good. I'm glad you're not there every day. Although I read in this morning's paper about poor Dwight Bower being killed in his office, so I guess it isn't only the museum. We all need to be careful anywhere we go."

"True. But you would think the murders are linked, so it must have something to do with Vivian or the museum."

"I agree." He hesitated. "I was thinking about Dale Jones. Do you know him? The woodworker?"

"Yes. His wife works at the museum."

"Imani. Nice girl. Had her in my freshman composition class several years ago. Anyway, I saw Dale leaving the museum early the morning of the murder. He looked so upset that I wondered later if perhaps he had some encounter with the same person who killed Vivian."

I looked over at the professor. "You saw Dale coming out of the museum?"

"I did. I'm sure he had nothing to do with the murder, of course. Such a nice, polite young man. But I wonder if he might have seen something or someone and not even realized a connection to the murder."

"Uh, that could be the case." Although, if so, I would have expected Dale to say something when I talked with him and Imani about her involvement.

Instead, neither of them had said a word. Imani had taken me in the workshop, away from Dale, and shown me the crib. Was that all done on purpose, to throw me off the scent? And what about the wood chip on the floor of my office? Granted, it could have gotten stuck on Imani's sweater and fallen off the morning of the murder. It could have been stuck on another sweater, another day.

Or it could have been left by Dale the morning of the murder.

A chill ran down my spine. "It might be worth calling

the police station and mentioning it to the detective. That way he could ask Dale if he saw anything."

"Exactly what I was thinking this morning as I ate my Grape Nuts." Professor Melkins nodded. "I'll call the station as soon as I return from my morning walk."

"In the meantime, I, uh, I wouldn't say anything to anyone else. You know how rumors spread in this town. You wouldn't want the killer to have any reason to come after you."

"Certainly not!" He jiggled the handle of his cane. "I wouldn't be able to mount much of a defense with this thing."

No, he wouldn't.

And I needed to be extremely cautious as well.

But I was going to have a talk with Imani. Because clearly, she and Dale were hiding something.

I only hoped, for her sake and the sake of their baby, that they weren't covering up a murder.

Chapter Thirteen

MONDAY MORNING, bright and early, I called Imani and told her I wanted her to go back through the records for all the community events the museum had hosted over the past year and determine the three that resulted in the most new memberships. I arranged to meet her at the museum at ten so she could get some files from her office.

And so I could ask a few more questions about Dale.

Cleo was busy all day Monday, booked solid with haircuts and colors, but we agreed that my conversation with Imani would be safe if, unknown to Imani, Alice was also at the museum, listening in and ready to call 911 if needed.

Alice arrived at the museum door right on time at a quarter to ten. As she came in the building, I noticed she was carrying a golf club.

My eyes widened.

"It's my husband's nine iron. He spent three hundred dollars on this club alone, and his golf phase only lasted one summer. I thought at least I could get some value out of it by using it for protection."

"Not a bad idea, although I still can't see Imani as the killer."

"Me either, but I'm not totally sure about Dale, especially after what you said when you called."

I unlocked the back door of the museum and led the way in. "Hopefully, I'll find out soon."

Alice and I sat on a bench in a room that had once been the butler's pantry and now held a display about the first local school, back when Dogwood Springs had been called Silersville. The bench was out of sight from both doors, the perfect place for Alice to listen in on my conversation with Imani.

At five 'til ten, there was a knock on the back door.

I gave Alice's arm a squeeze. "Here goes nothing." I drew in a deep breath and went to let Imani in.

She stepped inside and looked around the conference room. "Do you really think it's safe for us to be here, Libby?"

She seemed nervous, but given what the detective had said about her time in drama club in high school, it could all be an act.

"I had the locks changed, and Alice and I are the only ones with a key. I locked the door behind you, so I think we should be fine." I led the way toward the stairs.

"Okay." She gave a jerky nod. "And I'm happy to work on whatever you think I can take home. Both Dale and I like that idea a lot better than me being here in person. At least until the killer is caught."

"Speaking of Dale..." I stopped on the first step where Alice could easily hear, and I turned to face Imani. "What was he doing here early the morning Vivian was killed?"

Her face stiffened. "Uh, just dropping me off."

"Really? Then why did someone see him leaving the building? And why did the two of you conveniently forget to mention that he'd been here when I talked with you at your shop?"

"Uh, uh..." She covered her mouth with one hand and backed away from me.

"I want to believe you, Imani, when you say you had nothing to do with the murder, but you're clearly lying to me."

Her eyes shone with tears. "I'm sorry, Libby. I didn't want to lie to you. I was so upset and worried that Vivian would convince you to fire me, and then I had morning sickness really bad, and Dale was livid. Vivian always came in early, so he figured she would be here. He grabbed his keys and stormed off."

"Imani, if he's the killer, you need to go to the police. It can't be safe."

Her eyes grew huge. "Are you crazy? Dale's not the killer. All he did was yell at her. But he's afraid that if anyone knows he was here that morning, they'll suspect him. And from what we read in the paper, Dwight was killed Friday morning. I was at a doctor's appointment for the baby, and Dale was working alone in the shop. He has no alibi for that murder either."

She broke down sobbing, and I took her arm and led her into the alcove where Alice waited.

I knew I was doing the right thing, trying to solve the murders, but I felt mean. If this was an act, Imani should receive an Academy Award.

Alice pulled Imani onto the bench beside her and wrapped her in her arms. "It's okay, dear. You've been under a lot of stress. Try to take deep breaths and relax."

My stomach knotted. Was all the stress I'd put her under bad for the baby?

After a minute, Imani calmed down and looked up at me. "Do you believe me, Libby? I'm sorry I lied to you, but Dale was so worried. He kept saying that it would break his heart to be in prison when our baby was born."

"I believe you, Imani. I'm sorry I upset you. Are you feeling okay?" I pointed toward her abdomen.

"Thank you." She let out a huge sigh. "And I am okay. I think being pregnant makes me more emotional. I cried last night when I realized we were out of Double Stuf Oreos."

Alice patted her shoulder. "That's perfectly understandable. Your hormones are probably all over the place."

That did make sense. Frankly, although I wouldn't cry over it, I'd be sad to be out of cookies myself.

But we still didn't have a clue who the murderer was. "Imani, did Dale see anyone when he was here? Or a car in the parking lot or anything?"

"No, but he said Vivian finally backed down about firing

me, then she told him he had to leave, that she had a meeting at eight."

"Really?" All this time, we'd had no clue about that meeting.

Imani nodded. "I'm guessing that's the person who killed her because she was alive when Dale was here at about seven forty-five."

"You didn't see anything unusual when you got here at, what—?"

"Eight forty-five. No, I didn't see anything. But I didn't go near Vivian's office. I didn't want to risk making her mad by bothering her. I let Sam in when he knocked on the front door shortly after I got here. And I left the door unlocked because it was almost time for you to arrive."

I leaned back against the doorframe. "So, we have no clue at all who Vivian was meeting, no idea who could have killed her." I angled my head toward the entryway. "Let's go get those files, Imani. You can go through them at home."

My chest was heavy as we headed up the stairs. For all I knew, having Imani collect this data was a waste of time. As long as the murders were unsolved and the killer remained on the loose, any attempt to boost membership was going to be a disaster.

That evening, after her late day at the salon, Cleo stopped by and found me with an open package of shortbread.

"Uh-oh." She gave Bella a pat and pointed toward a few

stray crumbs on my shirt. "How many of those cookies have you had?"

"Three." I glanced down at the package. "Maybe four." Or five, but I wasn't 'fessing up to it. I brushed away the crumbs and offered her a cookie. She refused, and I led her into the living room, where we sat down on the two ends of the couch, each of us angled with our back to a corner so we could face each other. I told her what I'd learned about Dale and let out a long sigh. "So, we have no idea who killed Vivian or Dwight."

Cleo bit her lower lip, slipped off her shoes, and pulled her feet up on the couch to sit cross-legged. "I haven't heard anything at the salon. At least nothing related to Vivian or the murders."

I raised one eyebrow.

"Well, I did hear a rumor about Terry, that lawyer who's on your board. Apparently, he's been having another affair."

"Another affair?"

"Yeah. He was involved with a woman named Celeste—she's moved away—about three years ago. It almost destroyed his marriage, but I guess he got his wife, Brynn, to forgive him."

"And now he's having a second affair? What a sleaze ball." I wadded up a throw pillow in my lap, trying to force away thoughts of my ex. "But..." I jerked my head up and quickly told Cleo about my conversation with Patricia. "She's the largest donor to the museum, and she lives in Jefferson City. She said she saw Vivian at dinner with a man who seemed uncomfortable, like he didn't want people to know he was with her. Like they were having an affair. That could have been Terry. And maybe he killed Vivian."

"But why?"

"Well, let's think about this." I hunched forward over the pillow. "If Terry and Vivian were having an affair and all was going well, it wouldn't make sense that she would want to leave Dogwood Springs."

Cleo nodded. "So, there must have been some sort of trouble. Like if Vivian wanted to end things or maybe had been seeing someone else, Terry might have gone into a jealous rage and killed her."

"Or if Terry wanted to end things, Vivian might have threatened to tell his wife."

"Ooh, that would definitely cause problems for Terry. Brynn almost left him the last time. If this was the final straw, and she divorced him, I imagine he would be hit hard financially. Brynn's the Pennington heir."

I leaned forward. "I had no idea. That's probably why he's on the board." With the trust Albert Pennington had endowed to benefit the museum, it made sense that one of his family would want a say in how the place was run.

"Probably," Cleo said. "Brynn's not much for social stuff."

"And—" Goosebumps formed on my arms.

"And what?"

"And Terry's the one who made me think about life insurance, which made me suspect Phil. He said something about beneficiaries at the emergency board meeting."

"What did he say?"

"Nothing big, just a subtle comment. But Terry's a trial lawyer and probably doesn't make comments by accident. I bet he said that on purpose. And I bet he made a similar comment to Detective Harper, which prompted him to search Phil's house for clues—"

"And Terry killed Dwight because Dwight somehow figured things out," Cleo said quickly. "Maybe he saw Terry leave the museum the morning of the murder and was stupid enough to mention it."

"He wouldn't even have needed to threaten Terry, just say something like 'Wow, you could have gotten killed too.' If Terry knew that Dwight knew he'd been at the museum, he might have feared that the detective would eventually learn that and figure things out."

"That makes sense," Cleo said. "But how are you going to prove any of that?"

I let out a loud groan. "I have no idea. I'm certainly not going to confront Terry and try to trick him into confessing. He'd see right through me. All I can do, I guess, is go back over all the clues tomorrow and try to find something I can take to the police, something John Harper will believe."

"This detective business is complicated." Cleo stood. "I'm too tired to figure anything else out. I better head upstairs."

I picked up the pepper spray from where I now kept it on the counter, took Bella out, then got ready for bed. But I tossed and turned for hours.

We might have solved the case, but we had no way to prove it.

The next morning, I stared long and hard at my tea mug. In my mind, I could justify my sleuthing as helping the museum, but I had no idea how to find evidence to convince the police that Terry was the killer.

And if there was nothing further I could do to find the killer, I should do real work for the museum. I needed to finish up that grant proposal. To do that, I needed some paper files that were in my office. But despite the fact that Alice and I were the only ones with keys, the idea of being alone in the museum made my skin crawl. I took one last sip of tea, then called Alice and explained my situation.

"Would it be okay, do you think, for me to take Bella with me to the museum? She's very well behaved. She'd be in my office, not down with the displays."

"I think it would be fine. The museum isn't open, so visitors can't complain. And it's not as if we've never had a dog in there. We let service animals in the building."

Excellent. I thanked Alice and explained the plan to Bella, telling her to be on her best behavior. Then I packed her water bowl and some kibble for her lunch. And I finally remembered to put the Harry Truman bust in my bag.

I got a bit uneasy about the plan to take Bella to the museum when we had another squirrel incident, complete with loud barking, on our way downtown. But eventually, she acknowledged my gentle tugging on her leash and allowed the squirrel to continue terrorizing Elm Street.

Once we arrived at the museum, I grabbed the nine iron

that Alice had forgotten by the front door and checked every nook and cranny with Bella at my side.

Paranoid?

Maybe.

But my pulse was less jumpy when I returned to the front hall and leaned the golf club in the same spot, right by the front door.

In my office, the fingerprint powder had been cleaned away and the damaged chair was gone. A fancy new chair, complete with a big red bow and a tag that said it was from Alice, sat in its place. I sat in it, gave it a spin, then called her again, thanked her profusely, and told her the chair was perfect.

I pulled my laptop out of my bag and was turning it on when I had an idea.

Before I got to work on the grant, I'd open each of Vivian's files, not just the one that had a name that sounded suspicious. If Terry was the killer, maybe Vivian had evidence on him like she had on Dwight.

Three hours later, I took Bella out the back door, locked it behind me, and picked up a carryout salad from the café to take back to the museum. Another hour and a half later, I opened the last file in Vivian's account and blew out a frustrated breath. Like every other file besides the one named "Madoff," it was exactly what it said it was. I'd learned a lot about the past operations of the museum, but I was no closer to being able to prove Terry was the killer. And I'd wasted hours and hours.

But maybe Vivian didn't hide the evidence online.

Maybe she went old school. Feeling rather foolish, I rapped on the walls, hoping for a hollow sound. I crawled under the desk and looked for a key taped in an out-of-the-way spot. Bella helped by crawling under the desk with me and licking my ear, but even with her assistance, I didn't find a key. I took each picture off the wall and checked behind it. I even pressed on the carvings along the feet and sides of the desk, hoping I'd open a hidden panel.

More time wasted.

Finally, I pulled up Vivian's online calendar, although I already knew what it would say. All the meetings she'd written down had been understandable except for that mysterious note the day of her murder about H.S.T. But who or what was H.S.T.?

I clicked my mouse, opening the calendar to the day of Vivian's murder. There it was. H.S.T.

Wait. I leaned forward, squinting at the screen. Her calendar didn't say H.S.T. It said "H. S T." No period after the "S". Interesting. Possibly, Vivian was typing quickly and accidentally omitted the period.

On the other hand, it could be a reference to Harry S Truman, who once told newspapermen that the period after the S should be omitted because he had no middle name, only the initial S.

Vivian, like any good historian in Missouri—or any historian like me whose mother grew up in Missouri—would know that his parents had used only the initial so that it would honor both of his grandfathers, Solomon Young and Anderson Shipp Truman.

Obviously, Vivian didn't have a meeting with Harry Truman. If I remembered right, he died in the 1970s. But...

A hit of adrenaline shot through my veins, and I grabbed my purse from the floor. I dug deep into my bag and pulled out the bust of Harry Truman.

I twisted it from side to side, examining it and—after promising out loud to repair the damage to museum property—I slid a fingernail under the circle of felt on the base. I peeled it back and peered in the opening.

Yes! I reached inside and pulled out a tissue. Cocooned inside was a silver flash drive.

Chapter Fourteen

VERY SNEAKY, Vivian.

My heart rate sped as I scooped up the flash drive and plugged it into my laptop. The flash drive held a ZIP archive. I clicked on it. Realistically, it could have nothing to do with Vivian's murder. The files could be financial information about the museum or personnel information. On the other hand, any second now, I might know why Vivian had been killed.

A box popped up on the computer screen requiring a password.

Undeterred, I remembered what Zeke had done and typed in "admin."

Incorrect.

I tried again. "Password."

Also incorrect.

Again and again, I tried.

Vivian.

Harry.

Truman.

Missouri.

Museum.

Dogwood Springs.

Every attempt was incorrect, incorrect, incorrect.

I tried several of the words in all caps. I tried upper and lowercase. I tried all lowercase. I even tried "Vivian" backwards.

None of them worked.

At last, I sank back against the chair. I texted Zeke, copied the ZIP archive onto my laptop, and tucked the flash drive in my purse. I collected all the paper files I might need to finish the grant proposal and carefully locked the museum. Then I dropped Bella off at home, got in my car, and drove to Zeke's house.

But even after he asked me everything I knew about Vivian, even after he looked her up on Facebook to learn her birthday and a whole list of personal details like her hometown that she'd filled into an online quiz, Zeke didn't have any more success than I did.

When his mom, Cleo's sister-in-law, invited me to stay for supper, I thanked her, declined, took the flash drive home, and set it on my dresser. Tomorrow, I would try calling a professional.

If Sam Collins could run a computer company, surely, he could crack a password.

∽

I woke the next day to a fast, rhythmic tapping sound. I peeked over the covers. One of Bella's legs was sticking out of her dog bed and jerking against the hardwood. If I had to guess, I'd say she was chasing squirrels in doggy dreamland.

I was about to burrow back under the covers when a ray of sunshine glinted off the silver case of the flash drive on my dresser.

It was too early to call Sam, but the answers might be right there, waiting to be unlocked, if only I had the right password. How could I go back to sleep thinking about that?

I let Bella out, took a quick shower, and fixed us both some breakfast. Then we set out on our walk.

For Bella, it was a big day. She got petted by five different neighbors, got a hug from a boy down the street, and spotted a rabbit. She froze and watched it intently, her whole body quivering, but didn't bark. Apparently, while bunnies were exciting, they didn't pose the same threat to the neighborhood as squirrels did.

For me, the walk was a time of mental debate.

If the flash drive did contain evidence about who killed Vivian, I may have inadvertently kept the police from finding it when they searched her office. The bust of Truman had been on my kitchen counter. I may have kept them from solving the case.

But would they have found the flash drive? With the way it was wrapped in tissues, it hadn't rattled, even when I shook the bust. They would have had to connect the initials in the calendar with the Truman statue, something that only came to me once I noticed the missing period after the initial S. How many people, outside historians, knew the details of Truman's middle name? I wasn't sure.

I jiggled Bella's leash, encouraging her to ignore a toad that had hopped onto the sidewalk and to continue our walk.

In the end, I couldn't change what I'd done. I'd taken the statue for protection, not to hide evidence. All I could do was move forward.

At this point, the logical thing—and probably the smart thing—was to take the flash drive to the police.

But I just couldn't do it.

My mother was stubborn. Her sisters, at least according to her, were even more stubborn. Although I was sure it was to a far lesser degree, I might have inherited the family trait. I couldn't bear to be so close to the solution and not figure it out. And I sure didn't want to look foolish in front of Detective Harper if my theory about the initials was wrong and the information on the flash drive turned out to be personnel files on Imani and Rodney.

"Bella, time to turn around." I gave the leash a slight tug, and we headed back to the apartment.

I got her fresh water, poured myself a glass of iced tea, and scrolled through the numbers on my phone.

I tapped Sam's name in my directory, then stared at the word Call. After a second, I drew in a deep breath and touched the screen.

"Sam? Libby Ballard." I put the phone on speaker and set it on the kitchen counter.

"Libby." A note of pleasure rang in his voice. "I was just thinking about you."

My heart did a little pitter pat. He was?

"I read in the paper about the second murder and how you found the body. That had to be horrible."

Oh, yeah. My heartrate eased back to normal. Probably a lot of people in town were wondering about me. And what was I even thinking? Romance was the last thing I needed. Tech help, that's what I was looking for. "Seeing Dwight dead was pretty awful." I took a quick sip of tea. "I really want these murders to end, but I'm not sure Detective Harper is ever going to solve them."

"It does seem to be taking a long time."

"That's, um, that's actually why I'm calling. I found this flash drive hidden in my office, and I wondered if it might have information related to the murder on it. When I tried to open it, it had a ZIP file that was password protected. I tried everything obvious that I could think of, and a high school kid, a nephew of a friend, tried what he called mining Vivian's social media accounts for information, but that didn't work either."

"Pretty smart thing for him to try, though," Sam said. "He should come talk with me sometime about his college plans."

I glanced down at the phone and ran a hand over the back of my neck. There was a good chance Sam would think I should take the flash drive to the police. "Um, you wouldn't, by chance, know how to get past something that's password protected, would you? I'd hate to take it to the police and waste their time if it's just a bunch of personnel files or something."

"A little detective work, huh?" He chuckled. "That sounds like something I might be able to handle."

"Really?"

"Yep. I can try the English dictionary against it. If the password is a real word, I should be able to unlock it quickly."

"What if it's a nonsense jumble of letters and numbers and symbols?"

"Then it's a lot harder. But most people are pretty lazy, so unless the person who hid it was tech savvy or really cautious, this will probably work."

A zing of excitement shot through me. "Thank you." I was sure he could do it. After all, Vivian had used "admin" as a password.

The sound of Sam clicking a keyboard came over the line. "I'm swamped today. I have class all morning, a thesis defense after lunch, and after that, I'm supposed to be the tour guide and dinner host for a candidate for a position in the department. But if you leave the flash drive with our administrative assistant, I can work on it late tonight."

Tonight seemed an awfully long way off. I wanted answers now. Maybe I'd be better off taking the flash drive to the police. Maybe they would find the password sooner.

I traced a squiggly line in the condensation on my iced tea glass and frowned. Would the police department in Dogwood Springs have someone who could figure out that password faster than Sam Collins, even if he didn't start on it until tonight?

Unlikely.

And what if it was just personnel files? I'd feel like an idiot. "I'll bring it right over, Sam."

"I'll call you in the morning to let you know how it went."

I thanked him, got off the phone, and picked up my car keys.

Once I returned from campus, I gave myself a stern lecture. That grant proposal needed to be finished, and the writing in it needed to shine.

So, I got a glass of water and sat back down at my dining table, eyes focused on my laptop. After a while, I got in a groove. Vivian was a good storyteller, and that was the key to writing a convincing grant proposal, so the structure of her writing had been solid. I'd added a few bits here and there, but mostly, the work was hers. On the other hand, she appeared to use commas like salt, sprinkled here and there with no good reason, which meant the proposal did need some editing. I fixed punctuation, rewrote a paragraph here and there, and dealt with some rather egregious run-on sentences.

None of the editing was that difficult, but the proposal was twenty-five pages, single spaced, and the day dragged by. Finally, I took Bella on a long walk, ate dinner while watching an episode of the British *Antiques Roadshow*, and went to bed.

The next morning, I checked my phone as soon as I got up. Not a word from Sam. The deadline for the proposal, though, was closing in.

Before I sent it in, I wanted to go over it one last time, on paper. Then it should be ready to submit, right on time.

When my ex-husband and I divided up our household, he got the printer. I had yet to buy a new one. I'd need to make another trip to the museum if I wanted a physical printout to review. Once I got the proposal printed, though, I could give it that last review, and use the postage machine in Imani's office to get it ready to mail. Two hours, max, and I could return home.

"Hey, Bella, want to walk to the museum with me again?"

Walk was one of her favorite words. She trotted over and, after I rubbed her ears sufficiently, she allowed me to clip on her leash. I hitched my big purse onto my shoulder, and we headed toward the museum, both of us enjoying the day. The sun shone brightly, the sky was a brilliant blue, and all the shops were open and bustling with tourists. The cafe looked packed, and every outside table was taken, including the one I already thought of as Bella's and mine in the corner.

After fifteen minutes, we arrived at the museum. From the outside, it looked a little forlorn with its "closed" sign. Hopefully, Sam's program would crack the password soon, the killer would be caught, and tourists would fill the museum and its coffers.

After we went in the front door, I locked it behind me, and just to ease my mind, I grabbed the nine iron. Bella and I walked through the whole museum, checking the restrooms and closets. The place was empty. I was being paranoid. Alice and I were the only ones with keys. I put the golf club back by the front door and led Bella to my office. She settled on the rug near the door, and I got to work.

A couple hours later, as I was sticking postage on the proposal's envelope, my phone rang.

Sam!

I quickly answered.

"Libby, I got in. The ZIP archive held three audio files, and they're definitely not related to museum business. Two of them are practically X-rated."

"Oh." My cheeks grew hot. Talk about embarrassing.

"The third one, though, I think is what you want. Do you have time to listen to it now?"

"Do I? I've been dying for you to call."

"Okay. Here goes."

Chapter Fifteen

SAM HIT play on the recording.

Static, then the sound of a phone ringing.

"What?" A man's angry voice.

"Finally. I don't appreciate you avoiding my calls." Vivian's voice was easily recognizable.

"I've been busy." The man again.

I stared at the phone. I thought that was Terry, but I couldn't be sure.

"Yeah, right, you've been busy," Vivian said. "Busy cozying up to your dear wife."

"We are married," the man said. "We're supposed to spend time together."

"You used to seem a lot more interested in spending time with me," Vivian said. "Until you got worried that your dear little princess might divorce you and you'd lose all your money."

Yes! It sounded more and more like Cleo and I were

right! Vivian and Terry had been having an affair, and he ended it.

"What do you want, Vivian? I already handled your divorce for you at no charge."

"The least you could do, after you dumped me, was to make sure I got a decent settlement out of Phil." She let out an audible sigh. "The thing is, I've been pricing condos down in Florida, and I have to tell you, I'm shocked. To get something decent is going to cost way more than I ever dreamed."

Silence.

"Terry?"

Terry. Excellent. She'd identified him on the recording.

He didn't reply.

"I'd be so much more comfortable leaving town," Vivian said, "keeping quiet about our affair, if I knew I could afford a decent place near Tampa. I don't need beachfront, of course, but I think a unit in a community with a pool is the bare minimum."

"You'll have to keep looking, Viv, until you find something in your price range."

She made a pouty sound. "Terry, you know I've got those two recordings of us in bed, recordings that I'm sure your wife would be very interested to hear."

"And I handled your divorce at no cost, just like you asked, so you'd keep quiet."

"I know you handle the family money and that Brynn would never even know if you contributed to my condo fund for Florida. A small bit of cash would make all the difference. Maybe two hundred thousand?"

"Two hundred thousand dollars!" Terry shouted. "Are you out of your mind?"

"Did I mention I took photos of your bedroom the last time we spent the afternoon there? You stepped into the bathroom, and I couldn't resist. Remember, when Brynn was visiting her sister? I'm sure she'd love to get the whole package—audio and photography. I mean, the sheets and blankets do look a little messed up…"

"You conniving little—"

"Terry, Terry, don't be crude. The price just went up to two hundred and fifty thousand."

"You—" Terry's words dissolved into a growl. "Fine. Two hundred and fifty thousand. And you swear to never, never mention our affair to Brynn."

"Thank you, sweetheart. I'm sure I'll find a great place in Florida now. The sun, the palm trees, day trips to the beach. It will all make it easier to forget the pain of ending our two years together."

"Whatever. But know that this is the end. Two fifty, and never a penny more."

"Of course not, Terry. Unless—"

"I swear to you, Vivian. If you ask for more, you'll never see Florida. I'll kill you before you even pack your car."

She laughed. "Now, Terry, don't be silly. I know you'd never kill me. But just in case, I recorded this call. One more piece of evidence for my collection."

He growled again and hung up.

The faint static ended, and Sam came back on the line. "I think we know who killed Vivian."

"We sure do." I sat back in my chair and tried to shake off the ickiness of being in what used to be Vivian's office. "Wow. I thought people in Dogwood Springs were so nice."

"They are. At least, most of them," Sam said. "Now that you know what this is, it needs to go to the police. I've got a meeting in a few minutes, but I could take it in later if you'd like."

"If you don't mind, I'd rather come by and pick it up. After the way John Harper dismissed my ideas early on, I'd really like the pleasure of delivering it myself."

Sam chuckled, and we arranged to meet in his office in an hour.

Remembering the crowd at the café, I called and ordered a quick takeout lunch, ate it in my office, and then drove to the university. I found a spot in the shade, and after opening the car windows and promising Bella that I'd be gone less than ten minutes, I walked to Sam's office. A student sat across the desk from him, but Sam beckoned me in and handed me the silver flash drive. "For the police," he said. "I think they'll want their own tech people to open it." Then he handed me a second flash drive, this one in a pebbly-textured cobalt-blue case. "This one's for you. It's got the unencrypted files."

"Thank you so much." I gave him a big smile. If the

student hadn't been in the room, I might have hugged him. Finally, the killer would be stopped, and it never would have happened without Sam's help.

I didn't want either flash drive to get lost in my purse, so I tucked them in the back pocket of my Capris, which had a flap that buttoned down. Once they were safely secured, I hurried out to the parking lot and was unlocking my car when my phone rang.

I pulled it from my purse and answered as I climbed inside. "Hi, Alice. You'll never believe—"

"Libby, do you know about the leak?"

"What leak?"

"I got a call from Flora. She runs the bookshop two doors down from the museum."

"Oh, I've been meaning to stop in there—"

"She said she went out to put something in her car and saw water running down the back steps of the museum."

I froze, one hand on the ignition. "What?"

"I'm afraid some pipe must have broken. I'm on a preschool fieldtrip with my grandsons, and the teacher really needs me to stay. Can you go check it out?"

"On my way." I hung up and started the engine. What a nightmare. Water damage was the last thing the museum needed.

It was only about two miles from the university to the museum, but the trip felt as if it took an hour. At every stop light, I drummed my fingers on the steering wheel and envisioned what might await me. It all depended on where the break was. Worst case scenario was a bathroom on the second floor. What if the water ran along some path between floors and dripped onto the display about women in Dogwood Springs's history? Letters from Great-Great-Grandma Elsie and a diary from one of the first women to live in the area were under a plastic cover, but my stomach knotted even thinking about them getting wet.

In the passenger seat beside me, Bella seemed to sense my tension. She sat upright, peering down the road ahead.

I sped down Main Street as fast as the tourist traffic would allow and whipped my car into the empty back parking lot. Then I leapt out, Bella charging behind me as we ran toward the museum.

Just as Flora had said, water ran out under the door, soaking the three small concrete steps, forming a small muddy spot in the gravel parking lot. How had this happened? I'd only been gone about an hour, and everything had been fine when I left.

I fumbled with the key, finally forcing it into the lock, and pulled open the door to the conference room.

Under the sink, water spurted out of a plastic line. It had pushed open one of the cabinet doors and was shooting out onto the kitchen floor.

Most of the water followed the slight slope of the kitchen floor, flowing across the linoleum to the back door. But some had to be running down into the basement where Imani stored extra new member packets.

I dashed across the room. Two steps in, water soaked through my black flats. I grabbed the shut-off valve with both hands and, with a mighty twist, stopped the water.

Then I stood back up and looked at the water at my feet in disgust. Once this mess was cleaned up, I needed to have a plumber go over the whole museum. Vivian's cheapskate approach to property management was far too expensive in the long run. We might have to replace the new member packets, not to mention the whole conference room floor.

"Libby."

My lungs froze in my chest, and I spun around. "Terry?"

"Such a good museum director, coming to deal with plumbing issues." He stepped in from the hall.

Holding a gun.

Chapter Sixteen

MY HEART POUNDING, I tried to back toward the door to the next room, but Terry glared at me and gestured with the gun for me to stay in the conference room.

Bella looked from me to Terry and back again, then lunged toward him, growling.

"If that dog bites me, I'll..." Terry pointed the gun straight at her, and his eyes narrowed.

Bella growled even louder.

"Bella, no! Come here!" I shouted.

Bella turned to look back at me, her eyes uncertain.

"Come here now!" I shouted again.

She growled once more at Terry but slowly came to my side. I grabbed her collar and gripped it so tightly my hand hurt.

"Aren't you two cute together?" Terry sneered.

"How did you—" I drew in a raspy breath. "How did you get in here?"

He let out a sharp laugh. "Easy. You sent that email to the board saying you and Alice had the new key. My mother-in-law volunteers with Alice at the hospital, and she's told me at least a dozen times that Alice is there every Friday."

That still didn't answer my question.

"Don't look so confused. It's simple. All the volunteers put their purses in the same locker. My mother-in-law's car needed repairs a couple months ago, and she texted me the combination so I could get the keys out of her purse. I went to the hospital Friday afternoon, got the shiniest key on Alice's key chain, and had a copy made out of town. I put it back before she even noticed." He rolled his eyes. "Vivian had that recording incriminating me, and I knew she'd keep a physical copy. She only used the cloud for work because the board insisted. I'd already searched her house, so I had to look here. I spent the whole weekend going through her office."

The floor wobbled beneath me. "You went through her —my—office?"

He let out a snort. "Yeah." He glanced down at his wet dress shoes, and his mouth twisted into a scowl. "If I'd found what I'd been looking for, none of this would have been necessary."

For days, I'd thought I was safe in the museum, and the killer had the key the whole time. All weekend, while I'd been shopping for things for my new apartment, he'd let himself inside the museum.

Inside my office.

Just like he had today.

My stomach churned, and I felt like I might be sick.

Somehow, I had to figure out a way to save myself and Bella. But if I tried to escape, he'd shoot me. If I let Bella attack him and she bit him, he'd kill her.

I scanned the room, looking for something—anything—that I could use as a weapon. But there was nothing close to me except a package of paper coffee cups and a bag of ground coffee. The coffee pot—which I would gladly have bashed Terry over the head with—was behind him.

"Give me the flash drive," Terry said.

My muscles went stiff. "What flash drive?" And how did he know that was what Vivian had hidden?

"Don't play dumb. Last night at dinner, that flash drive was all my daughter could talk about. Some weird kid that her friend Gwen has a crush on told her that you have a flash drive. That he'd been trying to figure out the password because it might have evidence about the killer."

My stomach felt even worse. *Zeke, you idiot. Why couldn't you have kept quiet?* "Fine. We never did figure it out. I'll give you the flash drive, and we can forget this ever happened."

Terry rolled his eyes. "How stupid do you think I am? You probably already copied the files, and you'll give them to the cops."

I shook my head and tried to act as if I'd never even thought of copying the files. I could give him the silver flash drive, keep the blue one, and he'd never know there had been two.

But Terry didn't seem to buy it. His face shifted to an expression of mock pity. "Sadly, Miss Ballard, you're the final loose end I need to tie up."

My throat tightened. "Tie up?"

"It won't be hard. I'll make it look like you were here dealing with a plumbing problem when someone broke in, stole everything from that small jewelry display in the front room, and killed you in the process."

"That jewelry isn't worth more than $500. I don't think anybody would kill for it."

"The thief wouldn't know how much it was worth. And you won't be around to mention it." He raised the gun and pointed it straight at my heart.

I shook so hard I had to gasp for air, barely able to breathe. I had no idea if this would work. But it was now or never.

I released my hold on Bella's collar and tapped her shoulder to be sure she was paying attention.

Then I jabbed a finger toward the museum's tiny back-yard, clearly visible through the glass door—

And yelled as loudly as I could. "Squirrel!"

Bella exploded toward the back door, barking at top volume, dashing between Terry and me.

Terry jerked his head to look at her.

I made a break for it, racing for the front door and Alice's nine iron.

I took three steps into the next room, but Terry caught the back of my shirt and yanked me toward him. "Not so fast," he yelled, his hot breath on the back of my neck.

Flailing, I grabbed the acrylic cover of the case that displayed items about Elsie. I spun and swung the cover toward Terry.

It made a resounding *crack* as it slammed into the gun, which clattered to the floor near his feet.

He lunged for the gun, still clinging to my shirt and pulling me halfway down with him.

Using every ounce of energy I had, I threw myself toward the display case. My collar ripped, and my fingers encircled the cool, mother-of-pearl handle of Elsie's hatpin. I gripped it as tightly as I could and jammed it into Terry's arm.

He let out a wail, released my shirt, and crumpled to the ground on top of the gun.

I yelled for Bella, ran to the front door, and grabbed the nine iron.

We scrambled outside, my chest heaving, just as two police cars pulled up, turned into the alley, and parked. Four officers jumped out and ran toward me.

Officer Tate looked at me with concern. "Ma'am, are you all right?"

"Terry Kramer's inside, and he's got a gun. He tried to kill me."

Officer Tate rushed Bella and me over to the bench in

front of the appraiser's office. Another officer raced around to the back of the museum, and two more went in through the front door, weapons drawn.

"Are you injured?" Officer Tate bent down, facing me.

"No." I dropped the nine iron and reached to lay a trembling hand on Bella's shoulder. "Just shaken up." Tears ran down my cheeks.

I leaned over, buried my face in Bella's neck, and pulled her closer.

She licked my cheek, wiping away a tear, then nestled against my leg.

Oh, Bella.

I thought I was doing her a favor when I adopted her, thought she was the one who needed me. But she'd saved my life. "As soon as we get to go home, sweetie, you're definitely getting a doggie treat."

She let out a soft woof, as if she understood every word. Then she gazed up at me with love, gave a loud snuffle, and settled beside me, her head across my feet.

I turned to Officer Tate. "How did you know to come to the museum?"

"Alice VanMeter called. She told us about the water leak and said the more she thought about it, the more the timing seemed suspicious. She thought you were in danger."

"You sent two patrol cars based on her hunch?"

"Detective Harper said that, with two people already murdered, we needed to take every tip seriously."

"I'm glad he did." I sank back against the bench and let out a ragged sigh.

A short while later, an ambulance arrived. Officer Davis came out of the museum and spoke to Officer Tate. "Kramer tried to escape out the back carrying a gun, but we caught him. He's got a gash in his arm and says he was trying to help with the leak when she attacked him with a dagger."

"It was self-defense," I sputtered. "And it was a hatpin."

The officers exchanged glances.

Officer Tate's eyes narrowed. "A hatpin?"

I nodded.

"Don't worry, Miss Ballard," Officer Davis said. "We've got him in cuffs, and we've read him his rights. We'll get him medical attention, but then he's got a lot of explaining to do. Most people don't use a handgun to fix a plumbing problem."

Officer Tate reached down and patted Bella's head. "Your dog here seems really nice, but we can't bring her into the station. How about I have Officer Davis drive you home and wait while you get her settled. Then he can bring you in to make a statement."

"Thank you." I reached in the back pocket of my Capri pants, felt the cover of the pebbly-textured case, and rejected it. I pulled out the smooth, silver flash drive and handed it to him. "And here. I think this has some evidence on it you'll want."

"Excellent." He looked down at my hand, which was still shaking. "That's adrenaline. Maybe you should sit here another minute or two."

"Good idea." I sank back against the bench, and a tingly

feeling filled my head. Not dizziness, more a sense of amazement.

I'd nearly been killed, but the murderer had been caught.

Chapter Seventeen

THREE HOURS LATER, after I gave my statement to Detective Harper—who seemed much more concerned about me than angry—Officer Davis drove me home.

Cleo, Zeke, and Alice sat on chairs on the front porch. The minute I got out of the car, they rushed forward, all trying to talk at once.

"I'm really sorry I told my friend about the flash drive." Zeke could barely look at me. "I told her not to say anything, but I guess she didn't think that applied to her best friend. And her friend's dad was the killer."

"I know you didn't mean to tip off Terry." I patted his shoulder.

"I'm so glad you're okay." Cleo gave me a big hug.

"I'm thankful John Harper took me seriously when I called." Alice hugged me as well.

"Me too, and I'm so grateful you called the police." I unlocked my door and let Bella out. After a minute, she trotted back to me. "And I'm glad Bella was there. Good girl." I bent down to rub her ears. "Good, good girl."

I fixed her dinner, then got the box of dog treats out of the cabinet. If I based my decision solely on my gratitude, I'd give her the whole box, but I knew that wouldn't be good for her. Instead, I took out two and put them beside her food bowl.

"As soon as you texted back and told me you were coming home, I ordered pizza," Cleo said. "It got here about ten minutes ago, and I've got it keeping warm in my oven upstairs. And I've made something to go with it." She stepped toward the door. "Alice, can you help me carry things?"

While they went upstairs, I got out drinks and put hot pads down to protect my new table. I handed Zeke some napkins, and he carefully folded them and put one at each place at the table, as if neatness might assuage his guilt.

Cleo and Alice returned. Alice placed a large pizza box on the table, and Cleo added a bag of chips and a bowl of guacamole. "My special guacamole. It's my signature dish."

"It's your only dish," Zeke said under his breath.

Cleo glared at him, then shrugged. "He's right."

Someone's phone dinged.

Alice pulled her phone out of her purse and read a text. "That was the handyman I called. He's repaired the pipe that Terry damaged, and Imani and Dale are there, salvaging what they can from the basement. Dale says they have it under control."

"Thank you, Alice. You're the best museum board president ever." What would I do without her?

We all sat down, and I opened the pizza box, gesturing for people to help themselves. I put a scoop of guac on my plate, as well as a pile of chips.

I loaded a chip and took a bite, then raised the rest of the chip in a salute. "Cleo, this guac is awesome." Pizza was fine, but in my opinion, Mexican was always better.

She made a show of patting herself on the back, then nudged my elbow. "Tell us how you managed to get away from Terry."

"And what all happened after you went to the police station," Alice added.

I slid a slice of pizza onto my plate, and between bites, I told them about my day, starting with the call from Sam saying he'd broken the encryption on the flash drive.

Zeke stopped eating. "You know Sam Collins? You should have taken the flash drive to him to start with. He probably thought it was pretty funny that a kid like me tried to hack it."

"Actually," I said, "he was rather impressed when I told him what you'd tried. And how fast you figured out Vivian's password on the server."

Zeke sat up taller. "Any idiot can guess 'admin.'"

"Even so, he wanted to talk to you about your college plans."

"Sweet!" Zeke wiped his mouth on his sleeve again and grinned from ear to ear.

Cleo handed him a napkin and gave him a pointed stare,

then turned back to me. "Did you learn why Terry killed Vivian?"

"Nobody told me directly, but I overheard two officers talking at the police station. Apparently, after Vivian and Terry's affair had been going on for more than a year, Phil started divorce proceedings. Then Vivian started thinking that Terry should get a divorce as well, so the two of them could get married."

"Which was never going to happen, was it?" Cleo rolled her eyes. "If he got divorced, he'd lose all access to his wife's money."

"Exactly. He tried to end things with Vivian, but she blackmailed him to keep quiet about the affair. Early last Monday when he met with her at the museum, she thought she'd raise the stakes in the blackmail game one last time. Instead, he threatened her with a gun to get her to hand over the evidence about the affair, and when she didn't, he shot her."

Alice's forehead crinkled. "But didn't anyone hear the gunshot? I read once that you have to fill out a lot of forms and wait a long time to buy a silencer."

"Maybe he already had one. His daughter said he had several handguns," Zeke said. "Or he could have bought it illegally. I'd guess someone who would murder two people and try to kill a third wasn't that concerned with gun laws."

"Ah." Alice looked a bit sheepish, as if she felt she should have thought of that.

I took a quick drink of my soda and continued. "So, after he shot Vivian, Terry searched her office until he heard

Imani pull in the driveway. He didn't find what he was looking for, which is why he stole Alice's key to the museum and went in the weekend after he killed Dwight. But he still couldn't find the evidence Vivian had on him because it was inside the bust of Harry Truman"—I pointed toward my kitchen—"which was sitting on my counter because I kept forgetting to bring it back."

Zeke grabbed another slice of pizza. "Why did he kill Mr. Bower, the CPA?"

"Dwight saw Terry go into the museum before the murder. He said something because he was afraid Terry might have been in danger. But Terry was afraid that eventually Dwight would figure it out. Or his wife would. And with the air conditioner malfunctioning at the CPA offices, it was so loud that no one noticed when Terry slipped in the back door and strangled Dwight."

"Okay, I get that he planted the gun at Phil's to try to frame him." Cleo's forehead crinkled. "But how could he know it would ever be found?"

I patted Bella. "He couldn't count on you, could he, girl?" I gave her ears a scratch and looked over at Cleo. "My guess is that he left a corner of the towel he wrapped the gun in sticking out of the mulch. Or made the mulch look really disturbed in that spot. He probably figured the police would search Phil's house eventually."

"Wow." Cleo ran a hand through her hair. As always, it fell perfectly back into place. "What Terry probably thought was just another affair ended up in a double—almost a triple—murder."

"I still can't believe you managed to get away from him," Zeke said.

"Me either." Looking back, it felt surreal. But thanks to Elsie's hatpin and Bella, I'd escaped.

"Do you know what will happen to him?" Zeke took a giant bite of pizza.

"He'll be charged with two murders," I said. "As well as trying to kill me."

"He'll be disbarred for sure." Cleo scooted a piece of mushroom that was trying to escape onto the center of her slice of pizza.

"I should think so," Alice said. "And I bet Brynn divorces him."

Zeke piled a chip high with guacamole. "Brynn's daughter said her mom has already called a lawyer up in Columbia."

"Good," I said. "I hope Brynn and her daughter are able to put this all behind them."

"That won't be easy," Alice said. "But Dogwood Springs will rally around them."

"Of that, I have no doubt." The people of this town were special. Look at how they'd stood by Jackie Bower, helping her with her bakery after Dwight's death. And look at how they'd welcomed me.

I took a long drink of my soda and gazed at the faces around the table. Cleo, who from the moment I met her had treated me like a best friend. Zeke, who had accessed the museum files in the cloud. Alice, who helped so much with the museum and sent the police when I was pulled into

Terry's trap. And Bella, who saved me and filled my new apartment with love.

I'd come to Dogwood Springs less than two weeks ago, feeling I'd hit rock bottom. My ex had cheated on me, divorced me, and convinced my former boss to eliminate my position. Most of my so-called friends back in Philly had made themselves scarce. And I'd taken a new job that— after my initial excitement about having any job at all— deep down I'd thought was beneath me.

What a difference two weeks and two murders could make.

Now, I realized that the Dogwood Springs History Museum might be small, but it could have a real impact on the local school children, the townspeople, and tourists alike. I could make a difference. What's more, I had a personal connection with the history of this town, a connection I hadn't valued highly enough. These were my people, and the history of Dogwood Springs was my history, a history I was eager to share.

More importantly, I'd been welcomed here. I'd heard tales, of course, of how insular a small town could be, how it could take years to feel like a part of the community. Not in Dogwood Springs. Already, I had people I could reach out to in an emergency, when I had a bad day, or when I had something to celebrate.

And I had Bella.

Moving here, starting anew, had been the right choice.

I hadn't expected it, but Dogwood Springs was the place for me.

"You know what?" I looked at my new friends. "In spite of the fact that there have been two murders, in spite of almost being killed today, I'm glad I moved here."

Cleo wrapped an arm around my shoulders and gave me a sideways hug. "We're glad you moved here too."

From across the table, Alice beamed at me.

Bella walked over and laid her head on my leg, her tail thumping against the floor.

Zeke nodded. "Yeah. Helping you find that information about the embezzling was cool. And I've learned my lesson. The next time you investigate a murder, I'll keep my mouth shut."

My mouth dropped open. "The *next* time I investigate a murder?"

One day, if I worked hard enough, Dogwood Springs would be known not only as the prettiest town in Missouri, but also as the town with the most fascinating history museum. But I didn't see myself investigating any more murders. "I don't plan for there to be a next time, Zeke."

"Bummer." His face fell, and then he shrugged. "Well, you never know."

Epilogue

THE NEXT MORNING, I put on my favorite green shirt, a black skirt, my pearls, and—since my black flats had been ruined—a pair of black sandals. I rubbed Bella's ears and gave her a hug, then shouldered my big purse. "I'll be back at lunchtime to let you out, sweetie."

She gave a woof of acknowledgment and stood by the door, watching as I headed for the museum.

Fifteen minutes later, I said good morning to Imani and Rodney, then walked into my office. I removed the Harry Truman bust from the desk and tucked it into the back of a drawer of the filing cabinet. Then I pulled three blue carnival glass vases from my purse and arranged them on the corner of the desk. There. A small change, but it made me happy. I'd bought the vases years ago, before I got married, and even empty, they always brought joy to my workplace. Tomorrow I'd bring in a few blossoms to fill them. It was time to start living life here in Dogwood Springs to the fullest.

And it was time to make plans for the future of the museum. I wasn't going to let the murders define the Dogwood Springs History Museum any more than I was going to let my divorce define me.

Jackie Bower was coming in later this morning to make arrangements to return the money her husband had stolen. Rodney had his proposal about display cases ready and an idea for a new exhibit he wanted to discuss. And Imani, Alice, and I were meeting in the afternoon to brainstorm ways to increase museum membership.

I was just settling into my chair when footsteps approached my office.

"Knock, knock?" Sam Collins stood in my doorway.

"Sam, come in." I gestured to the guest seat across from my desk.

"I heard about what happened yesterday." He sat down. "I needed to talk to you anyway, so I thought I'd come by and see for myself that you were still in one piece."

My breath caught. He'd come to check on me? That was unexpected. "I'm fine."

"Glad to hear it. I did enjoy our detective work, but I wouldn't want anything to happen to you because of it."

"Well, thanks, but I'm okay, and I appreciate your help with the flash drive."

"Any time you need help with anything, just ask." He gave me a long look, then smiled.

My cheeks grew warm, and I twisted my hands together under the desk. "Um, you said you needed to talk to me?"

"I thought you'd want to know. I took the painting to a restorer in St. Louis. It's definitely a Clayton Smithton, and you were right. It had been altered. The restorer has removed enough of city hall to see that there was another person in the painting, possibly an older sister of the first girl."

"Wow." So it was not just a valuable painting, it was a valuable painting with a mystery. And it was connected to Dogwood Springs. "That's incredible."

"I know. But he says he's seen this type of thing before."

"I'd sure like to find out who that person was and why she was painted out of the picture." Surely, I could find some resources at the museum that would help answer those questions.

Sam leaned forward. "Once I get the restored painting back, would you like to see it?"

"Definitely."

"Great." He stood, and his gaze caught mine. "I'll be in touch. Maybe we can go out to dinner and discuss whether the museum would be interested in the piece and, if so, how to find a third party to appraise it."

Tiny bubbles of excitement rose in my chest. "I'd—I'd like that."

"Talk to you then." He waved and walked out the door.

I sank back in my chair and covered a silent chuckle with one hand.

Sam Collins had asked me out on a date.

And I said yes.

When I first moved to Dogwood Springs, I had been afraid life in a small town would be dull.

Was I ever wrong.

Thank you for reading this book!

Are you ready to return to Dogwood Springs for another cozy mystery? Join Libby, Bella, and their friends in the next book in the series, SALES, SECRETS & SUSPECTS.

Exclusive reader bonuses! Join Sally's cozy mystery newsletter to:

•get the FREE five-chapter prequel to the Dogwood Springs series, BED & BREAKFAST & BURGLARY

•read bonus content for every book, such as a scene in Bella's point of view

•learn about new releases, and more!

Visit Sally's website at www.sallybayless.com/free-mystery/ to join.

Acknowledgments

After years of writing romance, I began this book as an experiment, to see what it would be like to write a cozy mystery. To my delight, I discovered that in writing mysteries I found my true home. I am so grateful to the many people who encouraged me and helped me with this, the first in what I hope will be many mystery novels.

Thank you to my family—my husband, Dave, and our two grown children, Michael and Laurel. You, who know me and my logical, puzzle-loving brain best, were the first to suggest I try writing a mystery. And, lucky for me, you kept suggesting it, pointing to my shelves of mysteries and my love of Father Brown and other BBC sleuths, even when I said that the conventional wisdom in building a career as an author was to stay in one genre. A special thank you to Michael, who not only answers tech questions to keep my business running, but also helps whenever I want to use anything related to tech in my plots.

Cathryn Brown, my author accountability partner, also helped convince me that conventional wisdom was not always right. She encouraged me at every step of my venture into a new genre and offered invaluable suggestions on the manuscript. I am so thankful to have her in my writing life!

I am also very grateful to two experts who taught me about the fascinating world behind the scenes at museums. Jennifer Hines-Bergmeier, Board Co-President for the Ohio Valley Museum of Discovery in Athens, Ohio, grounded me in museum organizational structure and (thanks to her own years of reading mysteries) helped me brainstorm ideas for possible museum-related crimes. Rachel Gibson, Vice President of Programs and Director of Education at Belle Meade Historic Site & Winery in Nashville, graciously answered my questions about working in a history museum, shared fabulous stories, and helped me build the character for my sleuth, Libby. Hopefully, I've portrayed things accurately. If not, any errors are mine, and I vow to learn and do better in my next book by visiting more museums!

My long-time critique partners, Susan Anne Mason and Tammy Doherty, brought their knowledge of story and fabulous word-smithing skills to help make this book better. I am blessed to have their help!

My beta readers caught so many things that had slipped by and made wonderful suggestions! Many, many thanks to Betsy Anderson, Debbie Edwards, Ken Edwards, Jennifer Hines-Bergmeier, Janice Huwe, Martha Long, Kim Mather, Carrie Saunders, and Stephanie Smith.

With a new genre, I looked for a new editor and a new cover designer, hoping to find experts in the cozy mystery world. I was fortunate to find real winners for both. Many thanks to Paula Lester of Polaris Editing, who did a fabulous job, and to Donna Lynn Rogers of DLR Cover Designs, who created the delightful cover!

Trish Long of Blossoming Pages Author Services proofread this book, taking care of so many tricky details. Thank you, Trish!

About the Author

After many years away, Sally Bayless lives in her hometown in the Missouri Ozarks. She's married and has two grown children. When not working on her next book, she enjoys reading, BBC mysteries, word puzzles, swimming, and shopping for cute shoes.

Made in the USA
Monee, IL
20 June 2023